"I was protecting you

"From yourself," Justine c[...]

"Yes. If I hadn't pulled back, there's no way I could resist touching you, and that would make it impossible not to have you." Sincerity and longing darkened Cal's eyes.

"You wanted me?" She was almost afraid to believe it was true.

He kissed her and whispered against her lips, "I've wanted you from the moment I first saw you."

"That's hard to believe. I've read about your dalliances. Every last woman was beautiful and perfect."

"No one is perfect," he said.

"The women you dated came pretty close."

He studied her. "Sounds like you're having second thoughts."

"Not really. I'm just giving you an exit plan."

"What if I don't want one?" He took her hand and lifted it to his lips. "In case you're still not convinced, I'll make this as clear as I know how. I want you more than I've wanted any woman. Ever."

* * *

**THE BACHELORS OF BLACKWATER LAKE:
They won't be single for long!**

Dear Reader,

Calhoun Hart is a workaholic, and his family is starting to worry about him. Only the chance to win his grandfather's classic Bentley makes him accept his brother's challenge to vacation on an island paradise for a solid month. But when a guy breaks his leg skydiving on the first day, what other choice does he have but to work? As long as he's on the island, he can still win the wager. But it will require an assistant.

And so Justine Walker limps into his life, her bad leg a constant reminder of a profound personal loss. She's the only qualified employee willing to work one-on-one with a boss who puts in fourteen-hour days. Although she was warned not to do it, the tipping point in her decision to take the assignment is the generous compensation package, enough to top off her savings for the business she dreams of opening.

After arriving at the island's luxury villa, she threatens to quit only once before getting Cal's attention. They set up ground rules and work goes smoothly, but it's the only thing that does. Because this is paradise after all, and it's the perfect place to fall in love if two people don't have hang-ups. And sometimes even if they do.

In *His by Christmas*, Justine and Cal spend a magical month together, more than enough time to fall in love despite all the emotional baggage of their pasts. I truly had a blast writing these two characters and hope you enjoy reading their story.

All the best,

Teresa Southwick

His by Christmas

—

Teresa Southwick

◆HARLEQUIN® SPECIAL EDITION®

Recycling programs for this product may not exist in your area.

ISBN-13: 978-0-373-62384-6

His by Christmas

Copyright © 2017 by Teresa Southwick

Printed in U.S.A.

www.Harlequin.com

Teresa Southwick lives with her husband in Las Vegas, the city that reinvents itself every day. An avid fan of romance novels, she is delighted to be living out her dream of writing for Harlequin.

To Susan Mallery.

Your amazing creativity is only exceeded by your generosity in sharing it. You've always charged forward with your arms outstretched, urging other writers along with you. I'm grateful to be one of them and even happier to call you my dear friend.

Chapter One

"I've had sex recently." Calhoun Hart hoped there was enough self-righteous indignation in his retort to make the lie believable.

"You are so lying."

"You don't know that."

Sam Hart, his older brother, stared at him for several moments, gave him a pitying look, then laughed. "I'd put money on the fact that I'm right."

"I don't need money." Cal was the president of Hart Energy and had plenty. "What I want is that classic car Granddad left you."

"The Duchess? That's never going to happen. And it wasn't personal. He said it needs tender loving care and that takes time. Which you don't have because you're always working." Sam shrugged. "And I'm the oldest. Get over it."

Cal knew he meant get over second-son syndrome. He would never be first. In the line of succession he was the spare to his older brother's heir. For as long as he could remember, if Sam was going somewhere, doing something, Cal wanted to do it, too.

Although not marriage, which is why family and friends

were gathered in a banquet room at Blackwater Lake's newest hotel—Holden House. Sam had just gotten married and promised to love and honor Faith Connelly, the town florist. The invitation had said Reception Immediately Following and apparently the groom believed it was open season on Cal's sex life since his own was in pretty good shape. And he'd never seen his older brother look happier. For once the thought didn't crank up his acute competitive streak. The truth was, Cal envied him.

"I'm over the whole car thing," he declared. It was another lie, but he was hoping the groom would be distracted and quit ribbing him about his missing-in-action personal life.

"You'll never be over it, little brother."

"You're only nine months older," Cal reminded him.

Sam straightened his black bow tie, the one he wore with his traditional black tuxedo. "And an inch taller."

Cal couldn't do anything about that, either. He blamed the combination of chromosomes, DNA or whatever it was that had resulted in his own light brown hair and blue eyes and being six-feet-one instead of six-feet-two or more. But the reminder was just as annoying now as it had been for his whole life.

"Sam, you're an ass," he said. "Tell me again how you talked Faith into marrying you."

His brother glanced around the crowded room until he found the beautiful bride dressed in a lacy, long-sleeved, floor-length white gown. She met his gaze as if somehow knowing he'd been searching for her and blew him a kiss. "I had a little help from a miniature matchmaker named Phoebe."

The bride's little girl. Cal couldn't deny she was a cute, precocious child. "What did she see in you?"

"Good question. Maybe she knew I needed her and

her mom more than they needed me." Sam was dead serious. "I'm adopting her."

"Even more reason to congratulate you," Cal said just as sincerely. "You really do have it all."

"And you don't," his brother needled him. "In fact, you're not getting any, either."

So much for having a moment. "How can you possibly know that? Are you stalking me?"

"Don't have to. I always know where you are. Working."

"So you're studying surveillance footage?"

"Don't have to do that, either, now that you've set up an office for Hart Energy here in Blackwater Lake." Sam slid his hands into the pockets of his tux trousers. "And, in spite of that, there was still some question at the last minute about you being here for the wedding."

Cal felt a little guilty about that, but negotiations regarding a parcel of land for a wind farm were going south and he needed to be involved. "I made it, didn't I? I should get points for that. I haven't missed a Hart wedding yet. Except the one ten years ago Linc didn't tell anyone about."

"True. And you're the last Hart bachelor. Here alone, I notice. Evidence that you work too much to have a life and a plus-one."

There was more truth in that statement than Cal would admit. "Who retired and promoted you to relationship monitor?"

Just then Katherine Hart, their mother, joined the conversation. "Calhoun, this is your brother's day. Be nice."

And so, Cal thought, just like in football, it was the retaliatory hit the official penalized, not the inciting one. "He started it."

"Sam—" The older woman stood between them, linking arms with them. She was ageless and still beautiful, even after raising four children. "What did you do?"

"I simply pointed out that Cal is a workaholic."

"Not exactly how you phrased it." Cal didn't miss the gleam in his brother's eyes, the one that dared him to tell her the disagreement was all about him not having sex in a long time. That would happen when pigs went airborne.

"You do work too hard," Katherine said. "I was seriously thinking about staging a family intervention."

"Isn't that a bit dramatic, Mother?"

"No." Her expression said she wasn't kidding. Not only that, she'd left no room for rebuttal.

That didn't stop him from trying to make an argument. "It takes time and effort to run a successful company."

"No one understands that better than me. But some things are more important."

Not when he was competing with Sam for the best bottom line of all the companies that encompassed Hart Industries. "Look, Mom—"

"No." There was that rebuttal stopper again. "Working too hard is a flaw of the Hart men. It's a trait that nearly destroyed my marriage to your father, as you both well know."

Cal was aware that his parents legally separated when he and Sam were hardly more than babies. Because they were so close in age, she'd always called them twins the hard way. His dad worked all the time and she'd felt isolated and alone. Katherine's one-night stand during the separation had resulted in her getting pregnant and his brother Lincoln was born. Against the odds, Katherine and Hastings Hart had reconciled and their union became even stronger.

"I'm not married," Cal reminded her.

"You were once, but you never will be again if you don't make changes in your life."

Cal had left himself wide-open for that one. "Look, I just wasn't very good at marriage."

"That's no reason to give up. It's like vegetables. One taste doesn't get you a pass from them. Your body needs them and they're good for you."

Kind of like sex, Cal thought.

"You'll wither and die if you don't get any." Sam's remark was a clue that he was thinking along the same lines.

"Seriously," Katherine said, "there are studies that prove married men live longer. I want you around for a very long time, not working yourself into an early grave."

"Come on, Mom. You're exaggerating." When her eyes flashed with maternal intensity, he knew that was the wrong thing to say.

"When was the last time you took a vacation?" she demanded.

He thought for a moment and drew a blank. "I'd have to check my calendar. Can I get back to you on that?"

"I already checked with Shanna and she told me you haven't taken time off since she's been with the company, so that's at least four years."

"You went over my head to my assistant about this?"

"You have a problem with that?" There was a warning expression in his mother's eyes.

"No. Just wondering." He couldn't believe she'd done research on him. "She's probably right. Excellent at her job."

"She's so good you never give her time off, either. She's tired."

"I have an idea," Sam said. "Give her a vacation and you take one, too."

"I don't need a break—"

"Recharging your batteries would be good for you," his mother interrupted. "Your father and I recently took a trip to an all-inclusive island. There were so many activities available, or you could just veg out on the beach, sit in a lounge chair by the pool."

"Doing nothing would drive me nuts." Cal could feel his stubborn streak kicking in. That was never good.

"You can do as much or as little as you want," she insisted.

"I'll check it out." Again, when pigs took flight. Hopefully that response would get her off his back.

But Katherine's eyes narrowed as if she was onto him. "You think I don't know you just threw me a bone and have no intention of doing any research on a vacation?"

"Mom, can we talk about this later? Sam just got married and I'm sure he has stuff to do at this shindig."

"He's right. Faith just threw her bouquet, so it's almost time for me to do the garter thing." Sam's eyes took on a calculating look. "But I think I know how to resolve Cal's vacation issue right now."

"I bet you don't," Cal said.

"It's like you're channeling me." His brother looked way too self-satisfied. "I think you should take a week off for every year of avoided vacation. So, I'll bet you that you can't go to that island and stay for a month."

"Of course I can. If I wanted to."

"Ah," Sam said. "Wiggle room. I knew you couldn't do it."

The tone and the words hit a nerve and started Cal's competitive juices flowing. "Why would I want to?"

"For the Duchess." There was a dare in his brother's voice.

"But you love that car," Cal protested.

"I do. But you're not going to stay on the island for a month, so there's no chance I'll lose the car."

It was like they were kids again, and Cal felt that honor challenge clear to his core. A double dog dare if he'd ever heard one. Plus, he really did love that car. It was a Rolls-Royce Silver Shadow and something that belonged to his grandfather, which made it priceless.

He stuck out his hand. "You're on."

"Excellent," Sam said, shaking on the terms of the wager. "Mom, you're a witness."

"I am." She pointed to the activity on the other side of the room. "Look, all the single men are gathering. Sam, I think you're being paged. And, Cal, go catch the garter."

"No way."

"I've been looking forward to this." Sam rubbed his hands together. "I'll throw it right to you."

"Don't do me any favors."

A few minutes later Sam removed the garter from his bride's leg and threw it over his shoulder into the crowd of single guys. Unfortunately, Cal caught the blasted thing. The satin-and-lace symbol of the next guy to walk down ball-and-chain lane sailed just close enough that he couldn't resist the challenge of snagging it. Damn his competitive streak. And he was pretty sure Sam had done it on purpose, to prove relaxing was too big a challenge for Cal, that he was going to lose the bet.

His brother was wrong, Cal thought.

The problem was going to be finding ways to fill his time for a month on an island. Or die trying. Really, what could go wrong?

Calhoun Hart broke his leg on the first day of vacation, so now he was going to work on the island. Justine Walker believed she'd drawn the short straw in agreeing to fill in for his vacationing secretary. But that was before she stepped off the plane and saw sun, sand, sea. And palm trees swaying in the gentle trade winds. That's when it hit her. Working in a tropical paradise wasn't like being the one who had to stay behind to manually blow a nuclear device and prevent an asteroid from wiping out Earth.

Technically she hadn't drawn the short straw anyway. No one else in the clerical pool at Hart Energy wanted to work with Cal Hart. In desperation, Human Resources made her an offer she couldn't refuse. Putting up with the infamous workaholic who signed her paycheck meant she was that much closer to being her own boss.

Pulling a carry-on bag behind her, she limped up the flower- and shrub-lined path to Mr. Hart's private villa at the resort. Her leg was as good as it would ever be, but long stretches of sitting still made it ache. In spite of the discomfort, she was grateful the doctors had saved it after the accident. She'd come a long way from wishing she'd died, too.

In front of the impressive double-door entry, she stopped and took several deep, cleansing breaths, counting each one to slow down her racing pulse and heart rate. It took more effort than usual, but she didn't usually go to work in a villa with a three-hundred-sixty-degree view of the ocean. The crystal clear varying shades of turquoise water defied words. It was one of those sights one simply had to see. The stunning beauty almost made her forget about the discomfort in her leg.

She inhaled one last deep breath, counted, slowly released it, then knocked on the door. While there was no expectation of a speedy response since her boss was an invalid, the wait dragged on long enough that she debated going for help. But finally it opened and the man standing there, propped up on crutches, looked the picture of masculinity, in spite of the white, no-nonsense cast on his lower left leg. For the second time since his private plane had landed, she found herself without words. He was very sexy and that was more than a little distracting.

She'd heard about him, none of it flattering, but had only actually seen him from a distance at work. He was very good-looking with his light brown hair and deeply intense blue eyes. The white cotton shirt he wore framed his shoulders and probably made them look broader. Only a hands-on examination would confirm, but the odds of that happening were lower than zero.

"Good. You're finally here." He backed up awkwardly and negotiated a turn. "Would you mind getting the door... um—"

She realized he was hesitating because he either couldn't remember or didn't know her name. "Justine Walker. And I don't mind at all, Mr. Hart."

"Cal."

"Excuse me?"

"My name is Cal. Short for Calhoun, and it will save time if you use it."

"Of course."

She shut the door and limped after him into a spacious living area. The plush white sofas had throw pillows in tropical ocean shades, and a light-colored wood floor seemed to stretch on forever to the sand and sea beyond, merging inside and outside. Overhead was a high-pitched wooden ceiling and several fans with blades that resembled palm fronds circulated the refreshing breeze coming through the open French doors. Beneath her low-heeled pumps was the thickest, cushiest area rug she'd ever felt.

"Something wrong?"

Justine dragged her gaze from the floor and looked

up at her boss. She might as well be honest. "I think I'm on luxury overload."

"Oh?" He looked amused.

"I've never been on a private plane before or anyplace like this." She glanced around, not bothering to pretend she wasn't in awe. "And a villa with that ocean view—the sand and palm trees. It's amazing."

With a sigh he lowered himself to the sofa that looked big enough to hold an extended family reunion and elevated his injured leg. "Feel free to look around. Your room is over there." He lifted one of his crutches and used it to point to a recessed doorway on the other side of the enormous area. "The valet has instructions to bring the rest of your luggage, and he'll use the patio door so you won't see him."

The Human Resources director at Hart Energy had explained the accommodations—the fact that this villa was over five thousand square feet and contained two very large, very private suites. Mr. Hart's injury limited his mobility and he preferred his assistant nearby to facilitate the work environment.

The subtext was that she didn't need to worry about any hanky-panky. After meeting him that was oddly disappointing. But the compensation for this assignment was so generous, she would have slept on a lounge chair under a tree if he wanted. Before she could check out her room, there was a knock at the door.

"That should be room service," Cal said. "Would you mind letting them in?"

"Of course." She walked to the door and felt Cal watching her. When she was tired, like she was now, the limp was more pronounced, but she tried very hard to minimize it. Because she didn't want to show any weakness in front of this man.

She opened the door to several hotel employees who waited with wheeled carts containing covered dishes. Stepping back, she let them move past her and set everything up on the coffee table, where it was easily accessible to Cal. He signed for it and the servers discreetly left.

"Can I get a plate for you?" she asked.

"Yes. Thank you."

She lifted silver domes from the serving dishes and saw there were multiple entrées to choose from, as well as potatoes, rice, pasta, green salad and fruit. And a sampling of chocolate desserts made her mouth water.

She filled a plate and brought it to him, then arranged eating utensils where he could reach them. "You ordered a lot of food."

"I didn't know what you like and thought you might be hungry."

"I am." How considerate was that? He worked hard and expected his employees to match his pace, but no one had ever said he didn't treat the people around him well. Still, she'd pictured a heartless beast, and this unexpected thoughtfulness was a nice surprise. After fixing herself a plate, she sat on the plush chair to his right. "How did you break your leg?"

"Skydiving." He met her gaze. "What happened to yours?"

"You noticed the limp." She'd heard about his attention to detail and the demand for it from anyone he worked with. So he wouldn't miss much. Still, she hadn't anticipated his blunt question. She should have. There was no reason not to tell him, but he didn't need to know she'd lost more than her runway-model strut. "Car accident."

"Ah."

She took a bite of fish and nearly groaned out loud, it was so good. They ate in silence for several moments, long enough that the need to fill it became necessary. "So, skydiving. You're one of those sanity-challenged, adrenaline junkie thrill seekers who jump out of perfectly good airplanes on purpose."

"Yes."

Thank goodness she wasn't drinking anything when he smiled, because it rocked her like a 9.5 earthquake. He was a handsome man even with a serious expression on his face. But the smile made a girl want to raise her hand and shout, *Over here*. Fortunately she didn't choke, spit or utter a sound to embarrass herself, but it took several moments to gain solid mental footing again.

"Apparently the parachute opened," she observed. "Or the damage would have been much worse."

"I landed wrong." He shrugged. "It was a clean break and the doctor assured me it will heal quickly."

"Good. Are you in pain now?"

"It's been several days, so not much."

Justine knew a thing or two about pain, but didn't push him. Everyone handled it in their own way, and she was curious about something else. This assignment was supposed to last for a month so it begged the question, "Did you have any other activities planned besides skydiving?"

"Scuba diving. Parasailing. Rock climbing. For starters," he said.

"Bummer. So why not just cancel the vacay? You've obviously changed your plans and are going to work. Wouldn't it be easier to go home and schedule more time here when you're healed?"

Something that looked a lot like stubborn determination hardened his eyes and tightened his jaw. "The view is a lot better here."

"I can't argue with that." She looked through the patio doors to the luxurious, private, crystal clear pool, the pristine white sand and the ocean that stretched as far as the eye could see. "It's something special. But so is the scenery at home. The lake and mountains take my breath away."

He stared at her for several moments, then seemed to realize he was doing it. "So, you're part of the advance team from Dallas setting up the new office in Blackwater Lake."

"Yes."

She'd found the charming, rapidly growing town a good place to open her business. She'd been saving and moved to Montana with the idea of working there until she had enough start-up money. It never occurred to her that an opportunity like this would come along to speed up her timetable. Now that she thought about it, the offer had escalated because Cal Hart had a reputation for being difficult and demanding, and no one else who was clerically qualified had wanted it. So far he had not lived up to his advance billing.

Justine finished eating and set her plate on the table. "That was delicious. Thanks."

"Is there anything else I can get you?" he asked.

"No." She toyed with the cloth napkin still in her lap. "It was nice of you to think of this. Honestly, I wasn't expecting it."

"What were you expecting?" He didn't sound defensive, just curious.

"Everyone said you're a difficult boss who works twelve- to fourteen-hour days and requires your employees to do the same."

"You've been talking to Shanna."

"She's a friend. And having a lovely cruise, by the way." At his quizzical look she added, "Ships have internet. She emails. There was even one warning me not to take this job with you."

"Oh?"

"Yes."

"So why did you?" he asked.

"Do you have any idea what you're paying me?"

"A lot, apparently." He shrugged. "I can afford it."

She had no doubt about that. The question was, could she? He had her for a month. It hadn't occurred to her that four weeks in paradise with a man who wasn't a bastard and looked like a movie star could be a very long time.

Chapter Two

"So do you want the good news first? Or the bad?" Justine asked.

It was late afternoon on their first full day of working together, and Cal was stretched out on the corner group with his broken leg propped on a pillow. He glanced up from his laptop, focusing on his new assistant, who was sitting at the desk. Her red hair was parted on the side and pulled back into a messy side bun. She was wearing black, square-framed glasses that made her look smart and sexy, a one-two punch that had his gut tightening, not for the first time.

"I'm sorry," he said. "What was the question?"

"I've got good news and bad. Are you a get-the-bad-over-with-first kind of guy? Or a put-it-off-as-long-as-possible sort of person?"

"There's something to be said for both. So...surprise me." He'd been surprised by many things since she arrived yesterday. What was one more?

"I just received a preliminary environmental report on the wind farm property in upstate New York, and so far there's no negative impact on the animals, fish or ecosystem in the area affected by the project."

"Just a guess, but I'd say that's the good news."

"It is."

"And the bad?"

"The people aren't as open-minded as the wildlife. They're circulating a petition to squash the project." She slipped off her glasses. "The land is flat and the turbines are tall, visible for miles."

"They have to be tall. The higher they are, the more wind is harnessed." Even he heard the frustration in his voice.

"Protests are in the beginning stages. There may be some things you can do to sway public opinion and get everyone on board with this. Or at least the majority." She shrugged. "Can't please all the people all the time."

What could I do to please her?

Cal couldn't believe he'd just thought that. He was uncomfortable and it had nothing to do with his broken leg. Working with Justine was disconcerting. She was smart, efficient and seemed to know what he needed before he did. It had gone really well if you didn't count the part where he wanted to turn the lie about his active sex life into the truth. With her.

Redheads weren't even his type, but that didn't seem to make a difference. Maybe it was her eyes—brown with flecks of gold and green. They were different. Exotic. Mesmerizing and calm at the same time.

Beside him on the coffee table, papers were scattered around along with file folders and his cell phone. A half-empty coffee mug was right in the middle of the chaos, like a circus ringmaster. Her desk, on the other hand, was tidy to the point of making his teeth hurt. And it was time to get his head back in the game. There was a lot to accomplish, and one of her responsibilities was to clean up after him. Normally he wasn't quite this disorganized, but his mobility was limited with the cast on his leg. Work was why she was here in the first place.

"I'll talk to public relations about the protests and strategies to win over the people," he said. "Right now, I need you to pull together some alternative energy research. Statistics on the output of wind turbines at different heights. And reports on solar. There's a parcel of land I'm looking at in Nevada, and that's the place to go for sun."

Instead of going along with the directive, his assistant closed her laptop and calmly met his gaze. "I'm happy to take care of that for you in the morning."

Did he hear her right? Maybe the hard landing from his skydiving misadventure had broken more than his leg. "I'd like you to start compiling it now."

"If I hadn't already put in a full day—"

"We stopped for lunch."

"Yes, and it was incredibly delicious." Her look was sympathetic. "But I'm officially off the clock now."

Cal needed to get up and move. The urge to prowl was strong in him, but the plaster on his leg made it problematic, along with reducing the power of the pace as a means to show he was the boss and in charge. That was pompous, but having only one good leg threw him off his game.

He grabbed the crutches and hauled himself to a standing position, then hobbled over to the desk and rested his hip on the corner, letting it take his weight. This wasn't as effective as looming, but he could still stare her down.

"The fact is," he said evenly, "I'm always on the clock. There are pros and cons to being the president of a successful company and that's one of the downsides."

"So, you're saying that by extension your assistant needs to always be available?"

"Exactly. I knew you were smart." And not just another pretty face. But he kept that part to himself.

"Let me ask you this." She folded her hands and rested them on the unnaturally tidy desktop as she met his gaze. "Is it a matter of life and death for you to have that information this evening?"

"Hart Energy didn't get to be number one by not being prepared."

"That's not what I asked. It was a yes-or-no question."

Cal was hoping she hadn't noticed his evasive answer. Buying time, he studied her and couldn't detect a single sign that she was unnerved. Not a flicker of an eyelash, twitch of her mouth or jump in her pulse. This reaction was as unusual as the shade of her eyes shifting from brown, to gold, to green.

It *was* a yes-or-no question, but that was irrelevant since he ran the show. "It should be enough that I want what I want when I want it."

"First of all, that statement comes very close to temper tantrum territory." The corners of her mouth curved up.

The movement distracted him, drawing his attention to the delicate sensuality of her lips. It was several moments before he realized that she'd called him on his crap.

With an effort he pulled his thoughts together and kept his voice even when he asked, "And second of all?"

"Hmm?" She blinked.

Maybe he wasn't the only one distracted. "You said 'first of all.' That implies there's a second thing that you wanted to say."

"Right." She nodded. "If the reason you're asking me to work late comes under the heading of life and death, I'm happy to be flexible and accommodate the situation. Otherwise it's overtime and not part of my contract for this assignment."

"You have a special contract?"

"Yes. One that has very specific limitations on overtime. It was Shanna's suggestion after she advised me not to take the job. I could show you the agreement if you'd like."

Another yes-or-no thing that he was going to side-step. "So, it's not enough that there's more work to do?"

"There always is," she said serenely.

"I guess it's pointless to say that since you work for me you're finished when I am?"

"You're certainly free to continue working, but I'm off the clock. In the morning I will be at my desk and ready to give my all for Hart Energy. But to be at my best, I need to recharge my batteries."

Cal had a feeling she was laughing at him, and that tweaked him back into temper tantrum territory. Or maybe it was her calm, unruffled demeanor that made him want to ruffle her. Either way, something had him determined to get in the last word and maintain control.

"I would appreciate it if you would stay and complete the tasks that I've requested."

She stood and met his gaze, drawing in a deep breath and holding it for several moments. "I'm happy to work on it bright and early tomorrow morning. If that's not acceptable to you, feel free to fire me."

This was not a good time to find out the problem with temper tantrum territory was that it bordered on cutting-off-your-nose-to-spite-your-face land.

"Don't think I—"

She held up her hand. "Before finishing that sentence, you should know that no one else who is qualified for the position as your assistant is willing to come here and work one-on-one with you."

He would deny it if anyone claimed her words stunned him, but that was the truth. Did he really have a reputation for being a difficult boss? A workaholic? Apparently his family thought so or he wouldn't be in this predicament right now. Were they right?

Before he could come up with a response to the line she'd drawn in the sand, she said good-night and coolly turned away from him, heading for her suite. Staring at her trim back and shapely butt, he was again speechless, but for a different reason. It could have something to do with nearly swallowing his tongue. The woman had a body that would make a man follow her anywhere. Any man but him.

He couldn't decide whether to be angry at her audacity in challenging him, or in awe of her nerve and composure while doing it. She'd surprised him again and not in a good way. And another thing. Why had he pushed back so hard for her to stay tonight? She was right about the fact that the work could wait until tomorrow.

He refused to believe that it had anything to do with keeping her there so he wouldn't be alone. Lonely. He was either tired or just being stupid and didn't know which. Or maybe it was both. That wasn't a riddle that had to be solved right now and he resolved to focus on what he could handle.

He absolutely could get someone to replace her.

The next morning, Justine got ready for work. Cal hadn't fired her, although that was a technicality since she walked away before he could say much of anything. It was certainly possible that he'd fumed all night and was going to can her this morning—face-to-face. But she hoped not. She wanted to open her own yoga studio, and the dream was so close she could practically touch it.

She'd certainly thought it over all night and had no regrets about putting her foot down to keep him from walking all over her. If anyone knew how short life could be, it was her, and no way she was going to burn the candle at both ends for a paycheck. If he sent her packing she'd simply find another way to put together the rest of the money she needed.

And he was supposed to be on vacation, for Pete's sake!

She looked at herself in the suite's freestanding, full-length mirror. Her long hair fell past her shoulders, shiny and straight. For work she normally put it up for convenience, but she might not be working much longer. If a small part of her was using every female asset in her arsenal to get on the good side of her boss, well, so be it. That was, of course, presupposing Calhoun Hart even *had* a good side.

Her silky blouse was off-white, sleeveless and tucked into linen slacks that were long enough to graze the floor even in heels. No chance of showing any bare leg. Plus lightweight enough for this tropical island climate. And professional.

"I am woman. Hear me roar," she said to her reflection. "Meow."

With nerves jumping in her stomach, she exited her room and walked, head held high, as confidently as possible into the villa's main living area. It was early, but Cal was already up. In his khaki shorts and flowered shirt he looked like a tourist. The white cast on his left leg had her heart twisting with sympathy, proof it had not stayed strong and in solidarity with last night's rebellion.

"Good morning," he said. "I ordered breakfast."

Her gaze drifted to the covered dishes on the coffee table. There was an impressive number of them. "I should get to work."

"You should eat something first. It's the most important meal of the day." He poured coffee from an insulated pitcher into a second mug in front of him. "It's breakfast. Break fast. Fuel your body to maximize performance."

It seemed as if he was pretending their difference of opinion had never happened, and that was just fine with her.

"I'd love some coffee. Thanks." She sat in the club chair to his right.

"Cream? Sugar?" He met her gaze.

"No and no. Black is great." She took the cup and saucer he held out.

"I wasn't sure what you liked to eat and ordered a little of everything."

"That's getting to be a habit with you." She was teasing. Sort of.

But this showing his nice side was turning into a disconcerting pattern. She'd prepared herself to deal with the driven workaholic from last night, not this softie who was hard-selling a well-balanced, nutritious meal. This guy made her feel feelings she wasn't at all comfortable with.

"As habits go," she said, "it's not a bad one."

"Full disclosure. It's not entirely selfless, either." He grinned suddenly. "A well-fed employee is a productive one."

A smiling Cal looked younger, more carefree and less tense. And so handsome she could only stare at him. It was several moments before his words registered and the message was received. *Employee.* As in he was not going to terminate her. The weight of uncertainty lifted and she smiled back.

"I will be so productive that you won't be able to keep up with me."

"Is that a challenge, Miss Walker?" There was a gleam in his eyes now, a spark of competition.

"Absolutely."

"Then you're on. Eat up."

Since he'd ordered a little of everything, she sampled it all. Omelet, eggs Benedict, oatmeal and all the trimmings. But the fruit…mango, papaya and pineapple— yum. They ate in silence.

"So you like Blackwater Lake?" Cal finished the last bite of food and set his empty plate on the coffee table.

"Very much. It's beautiful." She met his gaze. "But I already mentioned that. There's a serenity about it. That sounds mystical and spiritual and I don't mean to be woo-woo weird, but peacefulness is in the air."

"That's because you don't have family there," he said drily.

"I wish I did. My parents, brothers and sister all live in Texas. They were not happy when I broke the news about the company headquarters moving."

"Would it help if I apologized to them and did a Power-Point presentation to lay out my reasons for relocating?"

"So it wasn't about being closer to your brothers and sister?"

"My parents are still in Dallas, too. So it wasn't an easy decision." Absently he kneaded his left knee, as if the muscles hurt. "There's still a large dependence on fossil fuels, but renewable energy is the future. It's my gut feeling that overseeing it from Blackwater Lake is the best way to go."

She wouldn't be with Hart Energy much longer and his commitment to its future made her a little sad about that. But that was his dream and she had one of her own.

"I can't eat another bite." She set her not quite empty plate on the table beside his. "And it's time for me to get to work."

"I left a list of what I need on your desk." His mouth

twitched, the only sign that he was thinking about their disagreement.

She stood and nodded. "I'll get right on it."

Moving away from the power of her boss's aura was a relief, and Justine buried herself in the familiarity of work. Reports, spreadsheets, phone calls and research meant she didn't have to think about the way a smile transformed his face, or how his teasing made her laugh. In the last few years laughter had been a stranger in her world. Changing that started with being her own boss, not bonding with her current one.

Four hours later, Justine was paying a price for burying herself in work. Her whole body was stiff and every muscle ached. Last night's mutiny hadn't been only about principle. Working long hours taxed her physically, and her leg needed regular stretching out to keep it from painful cramping.

She straightened in her chair and carefully stood, but couldn't suppress a wince of discomfort.

"Are you in pain?" Cal's voice was sharp, but that didn't hide a note of concern.

She'd thought he was engrossed in work and it surprised her that he'd noticed. That didn't mean she was comfortable with the fact that he had.

"I'm fine," she said.

"Don't do that." He looked and sounded even more annoyed, if possible. "You don't have to be superwoman."

To atone for pushing back against a fourteen-hour day. He didn't say the words, but they still hovered in the air.

"I'm not pretending to be anything. I really am fine. It's just that if I sit for long periods of time, my leg gets stiff and a little uncomfortable."

"I assumed you were kidding about competing work output."

"Yeah, but I also said I work hard while on the clock," she said.

"I appreciate the effort, but you should have said something." Now he sounded ticked off at himself.

"I just did. A fifteen-minute break to stretch it out will do the trick. In physical therapy after the accident, I learned techniques to take care of it. I'll be back shortly—more alert and productive than ever. And most important, it's relaxing. I'm used to this happening and know exactly what to do." She half turned, intending to disappear into her room to do what she needed to in order to loosen up the muscles.

"Don't leave on my account," he said. "In fact, I might need some of those techniques myself after this cast comes off."

Justine knew better than most that he had a point about life after his broken bone healed. Learning yoga during her physical rehabilitation literally got her back on her feet. The experience came really close to saving her life and the lesson was so profound, it changed her life. Or rather, her career goals. The dream to open her own yoga studio was conceived through her intense need to pay it forward and help others the way she'd been helped. How could she say no to this injured man?

"Okay," she finally said. "Just remember you asked for it."

She moved to a large area not far from the open French doors leading to the patio. She breathed deeply of the humid, tropical air, then released it. Turning, she saw that Cal was watching her closely, and her heart jumped. It was prudent to pretend that hadn't happened.

She kicked off her shoes and stood barefoot, facing him. "Normally for a session I wear stretchy yoga pants, so I'll have to wing it in this outfit."

"Do you want to change?"

"I only have a fifteen-minute break," she said to the man who'd gone to battle for more work hours. "It won't be a problem."

"Okay."

"I'm going to show you the tree pose."

"A tree doesn't immediately make one think of stretching," he mused. "Sounds a little like an oxymoron to me."

"Movements don't have to be sweeping and dramatic to make a big difference," she pointed out. "Just stand straight, shifting your weight to your legs and feet. Then bring your right foot up to your left inner thigh. In the beginning it can be challenging to find balance so it's all right to place your foot on the calf instead."

"And then?"

"Hold the pose and breathe."

"And this does what, exactly?"

"Strengthens your legs and back. Standing straight improves posture and works out the kinks from sitting at a desk for long periods of time."

"That sounded remarkably like a dig. Is it supposed to make me feel guilty?"

"Not unless it's working." She switched legs and grinned at him.

"Does that tree pose also turn a person sassy and sarcastic?"

"Just a happy side effect," she said serenely.

"Hmm. And you were preaching it as a relaxation technique."

"Indulging sass and sarcasm can be very relaxing." She finished the pose and had both feet on the floor. "Next we have the triangle pose."

"Sounds intriguing."

She ignored that and continued her running commentary. "This opens your chest and improves balance. Widen your stance and turn your right foot to the side, keeping your heel in line with the center of the left foot. Reach one arm out to the side, bend and touch the other to your extended foot. Again, hold and breathe. Repeat on the other side."

"And is that one relaxing?" There was a slight edge to his voice.

"Are you asking whether or not I feel a zinger coming on?"

"Not really." He shrugged. "I sort of figured that was a given. I'm actually getting used to it."

"Bracing yourself is not a relaxed way to be. For your own well-being, pay attention."

"Right."

"You're a skeptic now, but let's see how you feel when that cast comes off and one calf is half the size of the other because the muscles are atrophied from not being used."

"Have you got a move for that?"

"As a matter of fact...warrior one."

"Battle?" One of his eyebrows rose. "Seriously? I am actually more than a little skeptical of that being relaxing. Or helpful."

"Watch and learn, little grasshopper." She gave him a smirk. "This is for power and strength in the body. Stand straight, then move your left leg backward. Bend your right knee and turn your left foot slightly inward. Then raise your arms above you, stretching as high as you can, feeling that stretch into your fingertips. Hold and breathe. Again, repeat on the other side."

Justine lost herself in the pose, concentrating on her breathing and stretching. When she was finished, she felt refreshed and ready to resume working. The technique never failed to relax her. But one look at Cal told her the yoga lesson had the opposite effect on him.

His mouth was pulled tight and there was tension in the line of his jaw. But the expression in his eyes threw her completely off balance. Since her husband had died in the car accident, no man had looked at her the way Cal was now. As if he wanted her more than his next breath.

Chapter Three

There wasn't enough yoga in the whole world to make Cal relax after watching Justine stretch like that. Reaching up lengthened the lines of her body, showed off the toned muscles and put her spectacular curves on mouthwatering display. The lady had a limp and, in spite of that, she was lithe, limber and luscious. And he felt as if his whole body hurt from trying to pretend he hadn't noticed any of that.

The worst part was that he had no one to blame but himself. She'd warned him. He did ask for it. "Don't leave on my account," he muttered under his breath, thoroughly disgusted with himself. " I might need some of those techniques myself after this cast comes off."

The thoughts he'd been having ever since were inappropriate. He might be a workaholic, but he wasn't a pig.

Thank goodness she was done for the day. He didn't push the overtime issue again. No one could say he wasn't capable of learning. She'd been dismissed at quitting time but he continued to work. At least, he was trying. But after starting to read a technical report for the fourth time, he was about to throw in the towel. His mind kept wandering to the vision of that silky blouse outlining her breasts. The only thing sexier would be seeing her naked.

"Damn it." He rubbed his thigh and mentally smacked himself for more inappropriate thoughts.

What was it about her that was turning him into a hormone-overdosed teenager? Whether she was in the room with him or not, the place just felt different.

He glanced out the open French doors and saw her sitting by the pool in a patio chair, her back to him. Come to think of it, she'd been out there for a while. And as far as he could tell, she hadn't moved.

"None of my business. She's off the clock." He started at the beginning of the report. Again.

Almost immediately his attention wandered back outside to Justine's trim, straight back. She'd changed from work clothes into cotton pants and a tank top for her foray into doing absolutely nothing. Although he recognized the fact that it was a beautiful setting—the crystal clear pool, wicker furniture with brightly colored cushions and the pristine white sand in front of the sea. The sun was setting and turning the underside of the wispy clouds orange, gold and purple. But she continued to do absolutely nothing, and that had him acutely curious.

He grabbed the crutches resting beside him and pulled himself up, then propped them beneath his arms and hobbled outside. There was an empty chair beside her and he lowered himself into it.

"What are you doing?" he asked.

"Not working." She looked at him. "And neither are you, apparently."

"I'm taking a break." Ha. "So, seriously, what are you doing?"

"I'm looking at the sand, the ocean and that spectacular sunset."

"I don't mean this in a bad way—"

"Have you ever noticed that when someone says that, whatever comes next will not be positive reinforcement? It will be disapproving."

Guilty, he thought, then barreled ahead anyway. "You've been looking at the view for a really long time."

"It's worth spending a lot of time on taking it all in."

"Why?"

"Because it's stunning. The beauty of nature fills up my soul."

"Considering the length of your examination, can one assume your soul was that empty?"

The corners of her mouth curved up. "I'm filling the reserve tank. For tomorrow. You should try it."

"So you think my soul is a quart low?"

"Judging by the defensiveness of your tone, I'd say that's a very good possibility."

"Are you always this mystical?" he asked.

"Are you always this nosy?" she countered.

"Maybe."

"That's a lot of negative energy. Why don't you take in that magnificent view and think peaceful, healing thoughts?"

"What if I don't—"

"Just give it a try," she suggested.

"Okay." He set the crutches on the cement patio beside him and rested his injured leg on the chair's matching ottoman.

There was a refreshing breeze blowing off the ocean that gently rustled the nearby palm trees. The sun was an orange-yellow ball that seemed to be disappearing into the sea, and twilight crept closer, kept at bay by the villa's outside lights. Cal let out a sigh as some of the tension left him. It really was a pretty place. But…

"Aren't you getting bored?" he asked.

"No."

"How can you just sit there?" He studied her delicate profile and the beautiful fiery-colored hair blowing off her face. "I know you said you're filling up your soul, but how can you tell when it's sufficiently topped off?"

She met his gaze and there was amusement in hers. "It takes longer when there are interruptions."

"Do you set a timer?" he asked, warming to his cross-examination.

She ignored the question and stated the obvious. "You're restless."

"Because I'm not doing anything."

"Letting your body rest and rejuvenate is actually doing something."

"Doesn't feel that way," he grumbled.

"I have an idea. Why don't you try counting your breaths? That will give you something to focus on."

Besides her? When he could smell the scent of her skin in spite of the strong fragrance of tropical flowers and the sea all around? "Why would I want to focus on counting my breaths?"

"Inhale deeply," she instructed without answering. "And let it out slowly. Then concentrate on the rising and falling of your chest. Up and down is one breath. Give it a try."

"This is silly."

"There you go," she said. "I knew you would have an open mind."

"You're trying to spirit-shame me."

"Is it working?" There was laughter in her voice.

"Yeah, kind of."

"Good. Go with it."

"Okay." He did as instructed and drew in a deep

breath, then released it and noted the rise and fall of his chest. "One... Two... Three..."

"Silent counting would be better," she advised.

"Am I distracting you?"

"Yes."

Right back at you, he thought. She was the personification of distraction. If being a diversion was part of an employee review, she would get very high marks. Now that he thought about it, she was pretty good at her job, too. She worked very hard and was incredibly efficient. His vacationing assistant should be worried about the competition.

That was a bluff. Shanna was excellent at what she did, and the best part was that when she was in the office, he never once thought about her any way but appropriately. Why was that? She was attractive, single, smart and funny. What combination of attributes made Justine such a challenge to his concentration?

The only thing he could come up with was that karma had a lousy sense of humor.

"You've been very quiet." Justine finally broke the silence.

"I thought that's what you wanted."

"It's what you needed," she said mysteriously.

"That's news to me. And it makes you sound like a Tibetan monk," he added.

"It takes a while to get the hang of the technique in order to free your mind. But you did very well with the breathing."

He laughed. "Breathing is easy. If you can't do that, you've got bigger problems than filling up your soul."

"I'll make a convert of you yet. And I've got a month to do it." Justine got up and used the outside entrance to go into her suite.

Cal watched her go and admired the sexy movement of her hips in spite of the slight limp. His pulse jumped and his mouth went dry. There was breathing and there was heavy breathing. Justine could easily push him in the second direction. He'd teased her and she gave it right back, but he wanted her and it wasn't a joking matter.

This whole bet started when his brother needled him about his lack of a sex life. Right now the truth Cal had denied was painfully clear.

The next morning, Justine showered and got ready for work, still a little in awe of her suite and surroundings. She had as much connection to luxury on this scale as she did to a unicorn. Sand and sea were just steps away, for goodness' sake. The man providing this villa was also just steps away and he presented a whole different scale of excess. She really didn't know what to make of him.

When she'd lost her husband and little girl in the accident, it was the aloneness that nearly crushed her. Family and friends tried to help, but she had to fight through by herself. And she had, but there were reminders in Texas. When Hart Energy announced the move to Blackwater Lake, Justine looked at it as an opportunity for a change of scene and the chance to start a new life.

Physical therapy and yoga had helped heal her body and she'd resigned herself to being alone. Like last night on the patio. Then Cal had joined her and that had an effect. He'd actually attempted to master the conscious breathing technique. It was endearing, really.

Other than wanting everyone around him to work as hard as he did, the man was a good boss and very considerate. Too much of everything if she was being honest. Too handsome, funny, smart and sexy for any breathing technique she was aware of to relax her when he was nearby.

She studied her appearance in the bathroom mirror. "There's only one thing to do. Work hard and forget he's around."

Except they didn't work until after breakfast. Cal had given her the option of room service by herself, but having resort staff deliver two separate meals seemed excessive. When she walked into the villa's main area, breakfast was being set out on the dining room table. He signed for it and the staff wheeled away the cart and left.

Leaning on his crutches, Cal looked everything over, then met her gaze. "Breakfast is served."

"Good morning. It looks wonderful."

"It would be even better if you ordered something besides oats and dried grapes."

"Better known as raisins. And that's granola to you. I happen to really like it."

"You might want to consider expanding your culinary horizons."

"I will," she promised, then spotted the cup and saucer. There was steam wafting from the top. "Coffee. A girl could get used to this."

He sat at the head of the table. "Are you telling me that at home no one has coffee waiting for you in the morning?"

Justine took the chair at a right angle to his, where the bowl of granola waited. "Are you really concerned about my coffee consumption habits? Or is that a not-so-subtle query into my personal life?"

He lifted the metal dome covering his scrambled eggs, potatoes and turkey sausage. "The brilliance of my question is that you can interpret it any way you'd like."

"Hmm."

"Hmm?" he asked. "What does that mean?"

"It was either a noncommittal *hmm*, or a thinly veiled rebuke of your humility."

"You think I'm not humble?"

"When you call yourself brilliant? Duh." She couldn't help laughing at him. "And, just so you know, I'm going to answer what was asked. I take full responsibility for my morning coffee needs. What about you? Does Jeeves grind beans and brew the perfect cup of joe for you?"

"There is no Jeeves," he said. "I have no staff. A cleaning service comes in once a week to make the condo habitable."

"Condo." She poured almond milk into the bowl, then spooned up a bite of granola. After chewing and swallowing, she said, "I'd have figured you for a palatial country home kind of guy."

"There's not a lot of choice in Blackwater Lake. The town is growing and housing is struggling to catch up and stay current."

"I see." She sipped her coffee, studying him over the rim of her cup. "You're a complicated man, Cal Hart."

"Keeps people on their toes."

"People? Or women?" she asked.

"Women are people, too," he pointed out.

"And they no doubt fall at your feet. From all that brilliance, whether you're complicated or not," she teased. "In fact, I bet most of them prefer not."

"What do you prefer?" There was a deep, husky quality to his voice that could be called seductive. His eyes widened slightly and he said, "Don't tell me. Simple hard work is your preference. It gets the job done. Speaking of which…what happened to the contract my lawyer emailed? There are pages missing."

Apparently he was keeping this purely professional.

Hence the pivot back to work. That was for the best, even though she was enjoying their verbal sparring. "I know. It's on my to-do list. The internet was really slow, and then it just shut down."

"Damn it."

"I'm sorry. I checked with resort management late yesterday and they said the system can often be over-loaded with data."

"Then the system should be upgraded. If I was running this place..." He was buttering a slice of rye toast and stopped.

"What?" she prompted.

"Technology would be more efficient, for one thing." The frustration in his expression grew more intense as the muscle in his jaw jerked.

"Think about this place," she advised.

"I am. If someone is expecting some important documents or business negotiations requiring paperwork, their expectations will not be met."

"Unless this location is intended to cater to expectations other than business. Outside are sea and sand, neither of which is particularly user-friendly to computer circuits or memory chips."

"Of course not. No one's going to use a fax machine on a paddleboard."

"Exactly. People actually come here to get away from the rat race. To decompress outside in the water while soaking up the sun. Maybe upping their absorption of vitamin D while they're at it."

Cal glanced across the room, where the French doors were open to the patio. Outside, dark clouds had obscured the blue sky and were very swiftly rolling over the ocean toward them. Lightning flickered within the billowing black mass and a bolt zigzagged into the ocean.

"Great, just great," he mumbled.

Justine thought the approaching storm closely mirrored the expression on her boss's face. From the looks of it, he could use a refresher course in care and feeding of peace and relaxation. Something had him on edge. She hadn't missed the way he'd abruptly changed the course of breakfast chitchat from personal back to business. If she hadn't walked into this room prepared to work hard enough to forget he was there, she might not have noticed. But that was her plan of action and he'd gotten there first.

There was just one flaw in the all-work-to-avoid-play plan. And it was hard to ignore. "Cal, this is paradise. People come here to unplug. Technology doesn't have to be business-fast. It's not designed to do that. Probably so someone who's even tempted to choose work over relaxation will just give in and let it go."

"Try explaining that to my high-priced attorney who is waiting for me to look over that contract and get back to him. Strike while the iron is hot and all that. And there are other time-sensitive interests that are affected…"

A roaring sound outside made them both look out the doors. The storm had moved in really fast. Huge drops of torrential rain suddenly started bouncing on the patio, and the steady pounding was like the white noise on a sound machine. Then there was a crack of lightning and almost simultaneously the boom of thunder.

"It's right over us." The lights flickered and his expression grew even darker. "Paradise isn't perfect, after all."

"And yet, what most people wouldn't give to ride out an electrical storm on a tropical island as opposed to being at home."

"I'm not most people."

"Maybe you should give it a try," she snapped back. "Ordinary isn't so bad…"

There was another flash and the booming sound of thunder. Then the lights went out.

"Isn't that just swell?" Cal leaned back in his chair. "People, ordinary or otherwise, can't do much of anything now. Including work."

Justine glanced from the downpour outside to the irritated, angry look on Cal's face. "Wow. Bummer. Since the business machines are out of commission, you might have to sit here and talk to me."

"This would not happen in Blackwater Lake. And before you remind me the power can go out anywhere, I have a generator there."

"Then why don't you go back there?" That was a very good question, one she'd asked the first day and hadn't received an answer to. Call it the weird vibe of electrical energy in the air, but now she wanted to know. "Now that I think about it, carrying on business at the level you seem obsessed with is a challenge here. So, why didn't you go home after breaking your leg? What's going on, Cal? And don't tell me 'nothing.'"

Chapter Four

"But nothing is going on."

Pushing back against a statement of fact had put Cal in this predicament in the first place. You'd think he would know better than to keep doing it. Maybe he wasn't capable of learning, after all.

"Calhoun Hart, you're a big, fat fibber." Justine put her spoon down in her empty bowl. Her eyes narrowed on him and made him want to squirm, but he resisted the urge.

"I have no idea what you mean." He'd been about to say again that there was nothing going on, but decided it was protesting too much. He had to play this just right. "And 'big, fat fibber'? Really? Is this junior high?"

"And there it is," she said triumphantly.

"There what is?" He looked around the shadowy interior of the villa. "And how can you see it without the lights?"

"You're so glib."

Her tone didn't make the comment sound like a compliment, but that didn't stop him from running with it. "That just might be the nicest thing you've ever said to me."

"You tap dance pretty well for a man with a broken

leg." The words were spoken in a pleasant voice, but her eyes were still narrowed on him. "Your behavior is classic."

"How?"

"It tells me that you're hiding something." She held up her hand and started ticking things off on her fingers. "You turned the conversation back on me being 'junior high.' Then deflected to electricity. And tap-danced to twisting my words into a compliment. You better start talking, mister."

"Or what?"

"Now who's acting all junior high?" she accused him.

He grinned. "Then I'm going for it all the way. You're not the boss of me." Since when was being on the hot seat so much fun? The only variable was Justine. "There's nothing you can do to make me talk."

"Oh, you're so wrong about that. There are many, many ways I could bring you to your knees."

"One comes to mind. Using my crutches for a bonfire on the beach." He met her gaze and shrugged.

"There's no reason I have to be that cruel. Or literal." She tapped her lip. "I can think of a much quicker, much simpler way."

"What could be easier than commandeering a man's crutches?"

"I could call your mother." She smiled slowly and with more than a little wickedness.

"That's low, Justine."

"A girl has to do what a girl has to do." She pulled her phone out of her pocket. "I wonder if there's cell service during an electrical storm."

For several moments Cal wasn't sure that the pounding he heard wasn't in his ears. His sneaky assistant frowned at her phone and he guessed Mother Nature was giving him a reprieve.

"You can't call my mom. You don't have her phone number."

"Want to bet?"

He was beginning to wish he'd never heard the word *bet*. Little Miss Serene had a fairly ruthless expression on her face. Not unlike the stubborn set of her mouth when she refused to work overtime. She obviously wasn't going to let this go.

"All right. You win. There is something."

"Aha." She pointed at him. "So you are a big, fat fibber."

"Prevaricator. My vocabulary has improved since middle school."

"Then start using your words and tell me what you're up to. Pronto."

"Would you mind if I sat on the couch and propped my leg up for this?"

Her eyebrows rose. "Is it a long story?"

"There are some things I need to explain. All to give you context," he said.

"Well, we can't go to work until the lights come back on anyway..."

"Good." That would give him time to figure out how to say this so he wouldn't drain all the reserves her soul had so recently stored up.

Cal pushed to a standing position and balanced on his right foot while he grabbed the crutches and propped them under his arms. He swung himself over to the huge couch and sank into it, then put the injured leg up and stretched it out.

"Do you want me to bring your plate over?" There

was a spark of amusement in her eyes. "Keep up your strength for this?"

"Funny girl." He'd lost his appetite halfway through. "No. I've had enough."

"How about coffee?"

"Yes. Please," he added.

She ferried cups, saucers and the insulated pot of coffee to the table then poured refills for both of them. Taking hers, she sat in the club chair beside him and looked expectant. "I'm listening."

"Okay." He met her gaze and had the absurd thought that she looked pure and innocent even when threatening to tattle to his mother. Hopefully his confession wouldn't crush that out of her. "I'm a very competitive guy. Could just be my nature or where I fall in the family birth order."

"You're the second son."

Cal remembered his brother telling him to get over second-son syndrome. "So it's common knowledge."

"Hart Energy is a subsidiary of Hart Industries. If one works there, it would be hard not to know."

"I guess. The thing is, that's just a fact. It doesn't convey any of the reality of growing up in Sam Hart's shadow. We were born nine months apart."

"Twins the hard way," she interjected.

"That's what my mom always says. Anyway, I had the distinction of trying to keep up with him, pretty much right out of the womb. I wanted to do everything he did, including getting my parents' attention."

"This is where you own up to acting out."

He shook his head. "I did my best to be bigger, faster, stronger."

"Going for bionic?" Her mouth twitched, as if she was holding back a laugh.

"No, only first."

"Ah." She nodded her understanding. "And that could never be."

"I could never be firstborn, but in every other way I needed to win. School. Sports. Girls. We competed for the same ones."

A shrink would have a field day with the fact that he married a woman who had loved another man first. That man happened to be his brother Sam. Cal shouldn't have been so surprised and hurt when it didn't work out, but they said love was blind.

"So, your whole life has been like the second-place car rental company that has to try harder?"

"Yes. We run different companies under the Hart Industries umbrella, and I want him to be successful. I just want my bottom line to be better than his."

"That's why you work so hard."

"Exactly."

She nodded thoughtfully. "But that still doesn't explain why you didn't go home after breaking your leg. In fact, it just makes me more curious."

"I was getting to that part." As slowly as possible. He was dreading the expression of disappointment that he knew she would wear. The why of that was a mystery he didn't have time right now to think about. He took a sip of his lukewarm coffee, then set the cup back on the saucer. "It happened at Sam's wedding."

"It?"

"Apparently my family was concerned about the fact that I hadn't taken a vacation in a while."

"How long is 'a while'?"

"Four years."

"Wow. Long time." Her eyes widened.

"Then Sam made a crack about my social life."

"He thinks you're burning the candle at both ends?" she guessed. "He doesn't like your girlfriend?"

"I don't have one. And he—"

"Said something about you not having sex, which got your macho all in a twist. Am I right?" she asked.

"Not about the macho part, but the rest is pretty accurate. How did you know?" And why did she say it straight out without any awkwardness? Maybe because the lights were still out and clouds filled the sky. There was no way he could see whether or not she was blushing. It was one step shy of making love in the dark.

"I know because I have brothers. Two." She shrugged.

"Okay." He let out a breath. "His comment touched a nerve and then there's the classic car—"

"Just a hot minute. If this is you digressing to distract me, you should be warned that it won't work."

"That never crossed my mind." Because he'd already tried that and found out she was too smart to be sidetracked by his charming repartee. "It's important."

"Okay, then. Carry on."

"Our grandfather left Sam his classic Rolls-Royce Silver Shadow, even though I always told him I wanted it. He said it was about Sam being the oldest." Cal sighed. "I really love that car. But apparently Granddad told Sam that I worked too much to care for the Duchess the way she needed to be cared for. To make a long story short—"

"Too late for that," she teased.

He laughed. "Sam bet me that I couldn't stay on this island for a month."

"By 'stay' I assume he meant vacation?"

"That's not what he said," Cal stressed. "There was no stipulation about not working."

"But it was implied. That's the very definition of vacation," she insisted. "And yet you brought me here to help you work."

"I can't deny that."

There was the dreaded judgment in her eyes and it was definitely going against him. "That violates the very spirit of the wager. You're supposed to be here taking a break. Resting and relaxing."

Very little of either was going on, Cal thought. And it had only gotten worse since Justine showed up. "I honestly had planned to do that. I had a schedule of activities every day. A spreadsheet—"

"I'm sorry, what?"

"I had something on the calendar for every day. Parasailing, hang gliding, wave riding, rock climbing—"

Her mouth opened, hinting that she was appalled. "Those aren't gentle, peaceful or restful. They're life-threatening."

"I prefer to think of them as aggressive leisure interests." She was really putting him on the defensive. "The point is that I broke my leg on the first day and had to cancel everything. And I couldn't leave the island and lose the bet. Sitting around and doing nothing would have pushed me over the edge." He shrugged. "I figured that I might as well work."

"Wow. You would rather work when there's a beautiful, exciting island just outside the door to this luxury villa and it's yours to explore?"

"Not when you're on crutches," he retorted. "Believe me, I checked. No wave riding or parasailing when you've got a cast on your leg."

"You've never heard of plan B?"

"Of course I have. But, like I said, I'm complicated. And nothing fun is cast-friendly."

There was a gleam in her eyes when she said, "I bet

there's a lot of fun things you can do with that plaster on your leg."

"I challenge you to come up with a list of activities for a guy in my situation. Until then, don't judge."

It wasn't long before the lights came back on, the clouds disappeared and paradise was restored. Outside. Inside, Justine went to work, and when not busy doing something for her boss, she researched available activities on this tropical island. At lunchtime they took a break and she was ready with a list. After finishing a delicious meal of grilled fish, delicate rice, salad and the yummiest sugar cookies ever, she figured it was as good a time as any to bring it up.

She was sitting in the club chair beside the cushy sofa where Cal was stretched out. "I'm ready for your challenge," she said.

"Which one would that be?"

"I think asking the question is a stall technique, but we'll play this your way." She opened a file folder containing information she'd printed out. "There are many things to do on this island. Even for a man with limited mobility."

"Don't even mention the *W*-word."

She was drawing a blank. "I'm sorry. The what now?"

"Wheelchair."

"Ah." She nodded her understanding. "You're thinking limitations. My focus is broader. That's the difference between us."

"No. The difference is that my leg is broken. Yours are just fine." He stopped and that declaration settled in the air between them. "I'm sorry. By 'fine' I meant you're not on crutches."

"I know what you meant."

Her leg was fine if you were just talking mobility. It had taken surgeries, time and hard work to regain function, albeit with a slight limp, but the extensive scars would always be a visual reminder of what she'd lost.

"Moving on, then. No wheelchair. Got it." She scanned her paperwork. "You were right."

"I'm surprised to hear you admit that." But he looked puzzled. "What exactly is it that I'm right about?"

"Activities at an island resort heavily favor guests who are not in a cast."

"Like I said, there's nothing for me to do and I couldn't just sit around and do nothing. Hence the work. Given my circumstances, that's not a violation of the spirit of the wager with my brother. It comes under the heading of Circumstances Beyond My Control."

"Not completely true," she told him. "I said it favors noninjured people, but there's plenty to keep the physically challenged occupied."

"Such as?"

"Massage." She let that sink in for a moment. "The resort has a lovely menu of them. For example—the Swedish massage using long, fluid strokes to relieve muscle tension and improve circulation. Optimum blood flow will facilitate healing in your leg. And the technique will ease you into relaxation and relieve stress throughout your entire body. That's not just the spirit of vacation. It's proactive participation in it."

She looked up from her notes to gauge his reaction. There was a tight, tense expression on his face that wasn't exactly disapproval, but something that made her heart skip a beat. It was as if he could think of something *else* to relieve his body's tension, and that thought made her blush.

Looking back at her notes, she started talking, anything to fill the silence. "Here's one you might like. Vibrational massage using specially blended oils that vibrate with the frequency of the seven energy centers of the body to open and revitalize the chakras. This synergistic experience of breathing in each of the powerful aromatic oils, along with light massage, leaves you feeling balanced."

"Seriously?"

"Balance is good. That's why one takes a vacation. There's nothing wrong with working hard, but you need to offset it with play." She glanced up and saw amusement on his face. "What?"

"You know what they say. Your chakras can't be opened enough."

"Okay. Moving on." She flipped through the research. "Oh, here's something. Artistic palm arrangement."

"Basket weaving."

"Well…yes, but it would be helpful if you weren't an activity snob. The pictures of what people have done are quite impressive. And you can do it sitting down. All you need are two good hands and a yearning for artistic adventure."

"I bet thrill seekers from all over the world are just flocking to that one," he said wryly.

She nodded. "Good to know your chakras might be closed but your mind is completely open to possibilities."

"I'm glad you noticed." His voice dripped with sarcasm.

What she noticed was the way his smile and the gleam in his eyes warmed a path straight inside her and made her heart beat a little faster. Talk about possibilities. And no scenario in which she indulged them would end well. *Look away*, she told herself.

"I'll put you down as a maybe for artistic palm arrangement." She turned a page. "Now, this sounded like fun."

"Don't keep me in suspense."

She ignored him. "A cooking class specializing in cuisine from the island. As the description says, 'Extend your vacation by bringing home the palate-pleasing recipes for the foods that enhanced your leisure experience.'"

"Three strikes and you're out."

"You're determined not to be receptive to anything. I still won the challenge. There is stuff to do."

"It was a nice try, but work makes time go faster." He shrugged. "I just want it to pass so I can win the bet and go home to collect on it."

"That's just wrong, Cal. Do you have any idea how many people would give almost anything to be in your shoes right now?"

"You mean the broken leg, right?"

"That's just being deliberately obtuse." She stood and glared down at him. "You have the opportunity to be in this gorgeous place and the means to enjoy it—even with your leg in a cast. You're just feeling sorry for yourself, and it has to be said that it's not a good look."

"Oh?"

"No. You're determined to be miserable and bring everyone around you down, too. If you're going to win that bet, you have a responsibility to at least make an attempt to live up to the terms of it. Cheaters never prosper," she added. For all the good it would do.

"Are you going to rat me out?"

"As tempting as that is—no. You have to live with your dishonesty. Guilty conscience and all that." She shrugged and let the words sink in.

Anger, annoyance and amusement had all drifted over his face, but now he just looked thoughtful. "If you were here on vacation instead of work, with or without a broken leg, what would you do to occupy yourself?"

"I would sit on the beach in a lounge chair under a palm tree and read a book," she said without hesitation. "Parasailing or hang gliding would not be my first choice, in case you were wondering."

"I wasn't. And just so we're clear, if I tried to get to the sand, I'd get stuck." He nodded toward the crutches beside him. "And then there's the whole issue of getting sand inside the cast."

"That's the thing," she said. "Just steps from this villa's patio, there happens to be a lounge under a tree. You can make it that far and I'll help you get the rest of the way. Your bum foot will never touch the sand." It wouldn't take much effort, and Justine didn't know why she hadn't thought of it sooner. "What do you say?"

"I don't have a book."

"I can loan you one," she offered.

"Is it about breathing techniques and chakras?" he asked suspiciously.

"Actually, I can give you a choice. I have a romance novel or the action-adventure *High Value Target* written by Blackwater Lake's very own bestselling author, Jack Garner."

"I don't know—"

"Come on, Cal. Based on the schedule you had to scrap, you're not a man who shies away from a challenge. I can't believe you're afraid. What's the worst that could happen?"

"Famous last words—" But he swung his legs to the floor and grabbed the crutches, then stood and positioned them under his arms. "Well played, Miss Walker."

"That's the spirit. Your vitamin D is doing the dance of joy at the prospect of replenishment."

"That's something. It's the only part of me capable of dancing at the moment."

"Okay, then. Let me think this through. A good general plans out a mission. So, wait on the patio."

She hadn't considered the sand inside the cast and decided to put a fluffy beach towel on the lounge. Then she retrieved his sunglasses and handed them over before putting the book on the umbrella table anchored in the sand.

Moving back beside him, she said, "I'm going to set your crutches against the palm tree there. You can balance for a moment, right?"

"Yup."

"Okay. I'll be a human crutch. I'll put my arm around your waist and you lean on me."

"Yeah. I figured that part out."

She put the plan in motion, then moved beside him and slid her arm around him. "You're not in pain, are you?"

"I'm fine." His voice sounded deeper than usual, and it was usually pretty deep.

She wasn't sure whether or not he was just being tough but decided to take his word for it. "Can you hop?"

"Yes."

"Okay. Let's do this."

He was big, Justine realized. And solid. Not to mention warm and so very *male*. The thought put a hitch in her breathing. She hadn't been this close to a man since losing her husband and for the first time realized how very much she'd been missing it. She missed being touched, and a whole bunch of other feelings broke free and nearly overwhelmed her. But she couldn't think about that now. *Concentrate and don't let him fall.*

Fortunately Cal was athletic and his balance was good. He could have done this alone but she wouldn't let him. Because it had been her idea. They were standing in the sand by the lounge, and with his hand on her shoulder for balance, he maneuvered himself down onto it.

"Easy peasy," she said.

"Not from my perspective," he grumbled.

Justine was breathing a little too fast and chalked it up to physical exertion. Admittedly the sparks she'd experienced from touching him were a bit disconcerting. Other than that the strategy was successful.

"You're going to love this." She infused her voice with enthusiasm. "The sun. Wind in your hair. Looking at the ocean. When you're not reading, of course."

"Yeah." No enthusiasm.

"The best part is relaxing. No work. No talking about work." She sighed. "Heavenly."

"If you say so," he said.

"I do. Don't worry. I'll check on you. Just give me a wave when you want to come back in and I'll be back out to give you a hand."

"Excuse me?" There was disapproval in his voice, but the aviator sunglasses hid his expression.

"I have work to do."

"Not so fast. You're not going anywhere."

Chapter Five

"I'm not sitting out here all alone." Cal didn't care if there were dancing girls and acrobats. Justine had pushed him into this and now she was abandoning him? Uh-uh. Not going to happen.

"But you're paying me to do a job."

"I'm paying you to be my assistant. And I need assistance with this. Sit." He pointed at the lounge beside his. "Stay. Talk."

"But—"

"That's an order."

She didn't sit. "Seriously, Cal. There are things that I really need to get done. Be reasonable."

"I am."

"You definitely are not." She settled her hands on her hips.

Very shapely hips, he noticed. He sure would like to see her in a pair of shorts, or something besides loose linen slacks or long, flowing dresses.

"I think it's perfectly reasonable to request your company here on the beach." He looked up at her and realized he was enjoying this quite a bit. He might even go so far as to say it was relaxing.

"You said you were going to read a book," she reminded him.

"I don't believe I actually ever said those words. I said I didn't have one and you challenged my manhood by implying that I was afraid." He folded his arms over his chest. "Now, here we are. I think you're afraid to be alone with me."

"That's ridiculous." She huffed out an indignant breath. "We're alone all the time."

"Ah," he held up his index finger. "But there's always the structure of work to our aloneness. This will be different and I think that scares you."

"There are things I'm afraid of but this isn't one of them." She pointed her finger right back at him. "You're just being crabby and dictatorial. You realize that, right? A little while ago you were complaining about how slow technology on the island is and the pace was messing with work. Now you want me to sacrifice productive work hours to keep you company out here?"

"I've earned the right to be as crabby as I want. My leg aches. My scheduled activity plan is in the Dumpster. And the only assistant who will work with me seems to have a problem following orders." Her issues didn't appear to be with work so much as with him. "So, let me spell this out."

"Please do. I'm listening."

The words were consenting but that didn't fool him. Her tone was pure pushback. "There is no way you're marooning me under this stupid umbrella by myself. You pushed me into not working and there's a price to pay. Keep me company. You can put on a bikini if you want. I'll wait."

He knew she had a bathing suit because every night before bed she swam laps in the pool without the patio lights on. The dark was probably some yoga trick to eliminate nuisance and distraction so she could concentrate and push that beautiful body to peak performance. But the fact was, he didn't know what she looked like with fewer clothes on and would give almost anything to find out.

Cal watched emotions flicker across her face, ranging from stubborn to shy. And possibly scared. And darn if the freckles on her nose weren't as cute as could be.

"Really. You should put on your suit. One of us should take advantage of that beautiful, warm ocean. Or at the very least not get weird tan lines."

She sat on the other lounge, probably to shut him up. "I'm fine."

There's no way she was fine and he wondered about that. They stared at each other for several moments without saying anything. If she would start talking, maybe he could find out what wasn't fine. One thing he realized—it was far more interesting to wonder about her than think about the boneheaded choices that had landed him in this mess in the first place.

"So," he started. One of them had to go first and she showed no sign of cracking. "Say something."

"Is conversation with you in my job description?" She sat straight as a poker with her hands folded in her lap. Prim and proper, some might say.

For some reason that got his pulse pumping. Probably because he would very much like to find out the parameters of her prim and proper. "Talking isn't spelled out, but it's kind of implied."

"For work. Not this."

"I think the line between the two blurred when you bullied me into telling you about the bet." Cal was pretty sure that would get her to at least defend herself. He wasn't disappointed.

"I didn't bully you."

"Yeah, you kind of did."

"It would be impossible for me to push you into anything. You're bigger than me." Indignation looked good on her.

"Yes, but I'm fragile," he said.

"Oh, please. About as delicate as a charging rhinoceros."

"I think you're pouting and, quite frankly, I'm a little shocked by it. Didn't take you for a pouter." Cal continued to deliberately bait her, just to see how she would react. He wasn't proud of it, but since hang gliding wasn't going to happen, what was a guy to do? And maybe there was a little payback thrown in for good measure because she'd pushed him outside.

"Pouting? Me? Really?" Her chin lifted slightly. "I'm not going to bite. I'm made of sterner stuff."

And for some reason, that reminded him about her limp. "Tell me about the accident."

Again, her face was a kaleidoscope of emotions, which she quickly shut down. "That's not very interesting. Ancient history."

A swing and a miss, he thought. The lady didn't want to elaborate. "Then you come up with a topic for discussion. It was your rule not to talk about work."

"That was when I was going back inside to earn my paycheck," she said.

"I think we should take the rule out for a spin and see where we go." Because that left personal stuff up for grabs and he was very curious about her personally.

"Well, I've got nothing." Now her arms were crossed over her chest—classic defensive pose.

"Okay. How about this? We do questions. Back and forth."

She thought about that, then nodded. "I'll go first."

"I wouldn't have it any other way." He smiled and put as much charm as possible into it. "A gentleman always lets a lady go first. Hit me."

"Are you married?" she asked without hesitation.

The way she fired that one off, he would bet that had been on her mind, especially after he'd hinted at his pathetic social life. "No. Now me. What's your favorite food?"

The query was designed to throw her off balance because she would be prepared for him to ask the same thing. Judging by the expression on her face, the ploy worked.

Finally she answered, "Cookies-and-cream ice cream."

"That's not food."

"It might not be nutritionally well-balanced, but it is edible. Hence, food." Her mouth curved up at the corners. "It's an honest answer. I shouldn't have to defend it."

"You're right. My bad. There's no right or wrong here. How often do you eat it?"

"No you don't." She wagged a finger at him. "It's my turn." She seemed to be warming to the game. After thinking for a moment, she said, "So you're not married now. Have you ever been?"

"Yes." He could tell she wasn't pouting anymore and was glad about that. "I bet you want to know what happened, don't you?"

"Aha. That's your question. And my answer is yes. What happened?"

The stigma of failure didn't twist as painfully as it once had. "We got a divorce because I wasn't very good at being married, and I don't do things I'm not very good at."

She looked at the cast on his leg, then met his gaze. "So, no more skydiving?"

"An odd term for jumping out of an airplane when you analyze it. The words imply a soft, free-floating experience."

"And it is," she agreed. "Right up until you hit solid ground."

He winced. "Don't think I didn't notice you trying to sneak in a turn with that question. I believe the next question is mine." He was trying to think of something to ask that would get her to open up and give him more than a yes-or-no response. "How does your family feel about you moving away from Texas?"

"They're conflicted. We're close, so it's hard not having them nearby. But everyone also encouraged me to branch out and try a change of scene."

That was interesting, and Cal wanted to know why she'd needed encouragement to relocate. "So, you're making friends in Blackwater Lake?"

"Don't think I didn't notice you just took cuts," she scolded him. "But yes. I like the small-town feel and everyone is superfriendly. Why did you decide to move Hart Energy there?"

"Besides the fact that my brothers and sister are there, it's conveniently located with a lot of land for research and development. When the new airport opened, that sealed the deal for me."

"Why?"

"I travel a lot, and the closest one was nearly a hundred miles away. Now I have a place to park the private plane."

She frowned slightly. "Still, it seems a little surprising that you'd move to the same small town with the older brother you're still competing with. Aren't you trying to get out from his shadow?"

"Since our companies don't overlap, it's not him so much as leaving my ex behind." He'd been such a moron.

"Marrying her was a big mistake, but the stupidest thing was dating her at all."

"Why?"

"She went out with Sam first."

"Oh, my—" Her eyes went wide.

"Yeah. She loved my brother first, but he didn't feel the same and was honest with her, let her down as easily as possible. She turned to me for comfort and I thought I could come first with her. I was wrong, probably because she never stopped loving Sam."

"And you don't blame him for what happened?"

"No. I love my brother." Cal knew it was his own fault. Work helped him get through that difficult time and somehow it became a habit he couldn't seem to break. "The mistake was mine alone and one I'll never make again."

"That seems wise," she agreed.

Cal must have needed to get that off his chest, because she was extracting a lot more information than he'd intended. Turnabout was fair play.

"Okay, it's my turn. And I think you owe me about six questions."

"In your dreams." But she laughed. "Okay, shoot."

He'd run off at the mouth about his very personal life and stopped short of all the reasons he'd moved to Blackwater Lake. A major objective was to be close to his niece, and his sister, Ellie, was pregnant with her second child. He envied Ellie, her husband, Alex, and the beautiful life and family they were creating. The thought made him curious about Justine.

"Do you like kids?" he asked.

For a moment she looked as if all the air had been sucked out of her lungs. Then she took a deep breath and seemed to be counting. Then she said, "Yes."

"Care to elaborate?"

"No." The breeze blew strands of her red hair free, and she tucked them behind her ears. "Do you like kids?"

Maybe if he shared more information with her she would do the same. "I like them very much. I'm especially fond of my sister's little girl, Leah. Ellie is going to have another niece or nephew."

"Ah, because it's all about you." Justine smiled but it faded almost immediately. "Do you want children?"

"Hmm…"

She stared at him while he mulled it over and finally said, "That's a yes-or-no question, Cal."

"Not for me." He wouldn't take the step without being married, and his competitive streak had seriously messed with his better judgment. That made him reluctant to trust himself, so kids seemed unlikely. "It's a question mark. How about you?"

"Question mark." She'd kicked off her sandals and now wiggled her toes in the coarse white sand. When her gaze met his there was soul-deep sadness in her eyes. She shivered even though the tropical air was warm and humid.

He was getting a vibe and couldn't not ask. "Are you married?"

She looked back at him for several moments, and he doubted he'd get an answer. Finally she grabbed her shoes and stood. "Was. I'm starting to get sunburned. A redhead's skin and all that. Do you need help getting back to the villa?"

"I can manage."

"Okay." Without another word she walked away.

It took Cal several moments to realize that she knew a hell of a lot more about him now. But he knew very little more about her than he had before playing Twenty Questions. Something had made her sad and he felt bad about reminding her of it. Possibly it was the fact that she'd been married. Past tense. He also knew her skin was sensitive to the sun, but he was pretty sure that wasn't the only reason she'd called a halt to the game. She was running away from something.

Most women wanted to talk feelings until a man's head was ready to explode. Not Justine. Cal found himself in the unfamiliar position of wanting to know more. He was acutely curious about what she *didn't* say.

Later that night, Justine stroked and kicked her way from one side of the pool to the other. In the dark. She moved smoothly through the warm water, turning her face to the side to breathe. The same way she'd done since her first night here. She'd had no idea that Cal was aware of her evening ritual. And she wore a one-piece tank suit to do it, not a bikini, thank you very much. The exercise normally soothed her, but not this time.

Playing Twenty Questions on the beach had brought up memories and feelings of a life that seemed surreal now. Two years ago she'd been married to a wonderful man and had a beautiful little girl, but they died in the accident that nearly took Justine's life, too. The doctors saved her leg. If given the choice, she would have gladly sacrificed it to keep her family, but one didn't get to bargain or negotiate. Life and death didn't work that way.

Now she did yoga and swam laps to stay strong because nothing else made sense. And she was swimming those laps on a tropical island to earn money for her own yoga studio, to help someone else find the will to live like she had. For some reason she was still alive and clung to the belief that there was a reason. Something she was meant to do.

The thing about laps was that muscle memory took

over, freeing your mind to go wherever it wanted. Hers apparently wanted to go to Cal because that's where it kept ending up. Why hadn't he mentioned that he was aware she swam every night? And insisting that she stay on the beach today and keep him company. What was that about?

It wasn't spelled out in her work contract that she couldn't enjoy talking to her boss, and that was a good thing because she'd enjoyed it very much. He was handsome, yes. The sight of him was enough to make a girl weak in the knees. But he was also very smart. He really listened and remembered, so a person had better be careful what she said.

Justine was so caught up in her own thoughts that it startled her when the patio area suddenly lit up like a big-league ballpark. She swam to the end of the pool and grabbed on to the side. Cal was hobbling out of the villa and saw her watching.

"Hi." He moved closer and looked down at her, leaning on the crutches. "I'm sorry about the light. Just wanted some air and figured it probably wouldn't do my leg any good if I tripped over something in the dark."

"Of course."

"Hope I didn't mess up your yoga, breathing, Vulcan mind-meld meditation technique."

"What?"

"Swimming in the dark. No nuisance light or distractions to interfere with your concentration."

"Right. But seriously, the *Star Trek* reference?"

"You got that." He smiled. "Are you a fan?"

"Big time. The actor who plays Captain James T. Kirk in the new movies is perfect. You actually remind me of him a little."

"I'll take that as a compliment," he said.

"Just a fact."

"And it's a fact that you're swimming in the dark. Why do you do it?"

"It's beneficial after a long day of work." He started to say something but she interrupted. "This isn't about you working me too hard. I swim at home, too. At least, I used to in Dallas. It calms me and strengthens the muscles in my legs. And it's relaxing."

Although her nerves were anything but calm at this particular moment. She swam in the dark here mostly because she was self-conscious about the disfiguring scars on her right leg. This man had dated actresses and supermodels with perfect bodies. That was probably an unrealistic standard and didn't allow for photoshopping or body makeup. But that was her perception and that made it true for her.

She shouldn't compare herself or care what he thought but she did. That was obvious because she didn't get out of the pool. And even with all her physical therapy and yoga breathing techniques, she couldn't count high enough to breathe herself into serenity.

What was she going to do? If she got out there's no way he wouldn't see.

The answer was simple. She wouldn't get out. She'd keep swimming. A metaphor for her life.

"I'm going to finish my laps," she told him.

"Will it bother you if I sit here on the patio?"

"Not a bit," she lied. She pushed off from the side of the pool and started gliding through the water again. Back and forth.

His presence actually bothered her a lot. Not because he might critique her freestyle form, but her female one. If she was being honest, it was more than that. Just being around him had all her senses on red alert. There was something about him that made her want to say the right thing, be perfect. If she made him laugh, that made her feel so good.

Except vanity wasn't the only reason she hid her leg. If he saw the hideous marks and gouges out of the flesh from accident trauma and evidence of multiple surgeries to save it, he'd feel sorry for her, and his reactions would reflect that. He'd treat her differently, cut her slack when he otherwise might not have. All she wanted was to stand on her own two feet. Sink or swim on her own merit and not pity points.

So she kept swimming for as long as she could, but simply didn't have the stamina to outlast his apparent need for fresh air. If ever there was a time for strategic planning, this was it. When she touched the side of the pool farthest from where he was sitting, she pushed her shoulders out of the water and rested her arm on the side. There was a chair two feet away where she'd left a sarong and her towel.

She decided to hang here for a sign that he was going inside or was somehow distracted. Her hair was pulled into a knot on top of her head to keep it out of her face and she blinked the water from her eyes. Smiling brightly she said, "That was so refreshing."

"I can imagine." There was envy in his tone.

"Swimming will be good exercise for you when that cast comes off. It will build up the atrophied muscles in your calf."

"Wow, that sounds so attractive."

"Don't worry. It won't take long before you'll be back to impressing the ladies with your manly legs."

He laughed. "That will be an improvement since I never impressed anyone with them before."

Although she wasn't going to correct him, that wasn't

completely true. He wore shorts every day—to accommodate the cast on his lower leg, but also for the tropical climate. Along with the cotton flowered shirts, the look suited him. Justine liked his legs, muscular with a masculine dusting of hair. Even what she could see of the injured one looked good. Strong thighs. Unlike her, no one would stare at him because he was different, unattractive.

"It won't take long to get back in shape. The cast will be gone and you'll be off and running again before you know it."

"Time flies when you're having fun."

A breeze blew over her wet shoulders and made her shiver. Time was not flying nearly fast enough for her. There was no sign that he was going inside, so she needed a distraction and went with the best one she could think of.

"Is that your cell phone?"

"What?"

"I thought I heard your ringtone," she said.

He felt his shirt pocket. "Damn, I left it inside. Stupid since I've been waiting for a call from my attorney. His timing stinks."

The lie wasn't without consequences. Justine felt guilty and would have to live with it. She watched him stand, gracefully prop the crutches under his arms, then propel himself to the doorway. He was getting really good on them, a sign of his athleticism. As soon as he was inside she hauled herself out of the pool, grabbed the towel and quickly dried off. She was just tying the sarong around her waist when he came back outside.

"No one called."

"Sorry. Must have been water in my ears. Or the wind rustling the palm trees." She walked closer. Now that her leg was covered by the floor-length, flowered material, her confidence was properly back in place. "It's a pretty night, don't you think?"

"Yeah." He looked up.

"Without the nuisance light, the moon and stars are spectacular. And that's not a yoga thing. Just a fact."

"I'm aware."

Justine had been staring up at the sky, but the hoarse, slightly ragged edge to his voice drew her gaze back to his. There was a tense and hungry expression on his face, exactly the way he'd looked at her when she'd demonstrated her stretching technique.

Instantly her heart started racing as if she'd set an Olympic record in the one-hundred-meter freestyle. Her body had been so cold a few minutes ago and she'd been desperate enough to lie in order to get out of the pool. Now she was hot all over and the last thing she wanted was to move away from him.

Cal cleared his throat. "I'm going to try to get my attorney on the phone. It's still business hours in the States."

"Right."

A muscle in his jaw jerked as if he was clenching his teeth, and the tension in his eyes looked very near the snapping point. "I'll say good-night."

"Okay. See you in the morning."

Without another word he turned and went back into his suite, shutting the door behind him.

Justine stood there, thought about what just happened and waited for the wave of shame to pull her down because she'd felt something for another man. Recognizing survivor's guilt for being alive when her husband and child weren't didn't mean it would magically go away. She'd struggled with it for a while, even when everyone told her she had to go on living. That if she could change what happened she would. That her husband and child would want her to move forward and not live in the past.

Tonight, with Cal, she had her *aha* moment. She knew what they meant. It had been a long time since she'd thought about sex, but the way Cal looked at her changed that. He made her realize she had physical needs. So, why now? Why him?

He was her boss. Which just proved that fate had a warped sense of humor.

Chapter Six

So now he'd seen Justine Walker in a bathing suit. The problem was, what he *hadn't* seen kept him awake last night.

Cal was sitting on the large sofa with his leg propped up and his computer in his lap. From here he could watch her at the desk—reading email, going over cost projections and reports. There was the cutest expression on her face, the one he knew meant she was concentrating. So was he, but it had nothing to do with work.

A time or two she'd caught him watching her, and color rose in her cheeks. Did that mean she could read his mind? Because the fact was, he would really like to see her in a bathing suit. Technically he had but she'd been in the water and that blurred everything. And he wouldn't turn down the opportunity to get a look at her without that thing she put on as soon as she got out of the pool. That's not to say what he had seen wasn't top-notch. She had toned arms and a trim waist, but maybe he was an all-or-nothing kind of guy.

He wanted to see all of her and couldn't get the thought out of his mind. So he couldn't focus on much of anything except sliding those loose, gauzy pants off to find out if her body was as spectacular as he suspected. Just like that he was the sultan of slime and he wasn't proud of it. Enough. Time to get his mind back on work, and talking about it would be better than looking at a computer screen. That made it too easy for his mind to wander.

"What are you reading?" he asked.

Justine glanced up and met his gaze over her laptop. "A report on renewable energy from Las Vegas."

"And?"

"The city government is drawing one hundred percent of its power from renewable energy sources to run everything from city hall to parks, community centers and even streetlights."

"Impressive."

"Solar generates the energy to power on-site facilities with tree-shaped solar panels, solar shade canopies at city parks and solar arrays on rooftops."

"I'm guessing that because of its size the city can't get all the necessary power from on-site sources."

"You'd be correct." She removed her glasses and set them on the desk. "But the shift to renewable resulted in significant savings."

"Hmm." He nodded thoughtfully. "I'm going to talk to Mayor McKnight about doing that in Blackwater Lake."

"I haven't met the mayor. What do you think the chances are that she'll be receptive?" Justine asked.

"She's open-minded, so I think there's a fair shot. But she's a formidable woman." Not unlike the one in front of him. "There was a fire this summer that caused widespread evacuations. It was just before I moved into my condo, so I wasn't there yet. But my brother Sam said that in addition to coordinating state and local firefighting resources, Madam Mayor made sure everyone was housed with a family in a home and not in the high school gym."

"Wow."

"In fact, she's responsible for Sam getting together with Faith Connelly."

"Oh?"

"Sam has a big house. Faith and her daughter, Phoebe, needed someplace to go. Mayor Loretta gave him a little push, and while living under the same roof, the two of them fell victim to their tender emotions."

"Be still my heart. So what's the moral of the story?" she asked.

"What makes you think there is one?"

"You're so relationship-averse that you can't even say the word *love*. So there must be a cautionary tale in there somewhere."

"Did you just call me the love Grinch?" He closed his laptop. "And did you notice how I just said the word there?"

"No one will ever accuse you of being Cupid." She smiled. "And yes, I noticed."

"Okay. Fair enough."

"But, if you think about it—" she tapped her lip "—it's not an evacuation, but you and I are living under the same roof."

"For three more weeks," he pointed out. There was a time limit and that made it different somehow.

"How long did it take for Sam and Faith to fall for each other?"

"I have no idea."

"So, it could have been an hour? A day? A week?" She met his gaze. "Or a month?"

When had this conversation gone from him relating a pleasant anecdote to an inquisition? "What's your point?"

"I don't actually have one. It's just fun to watch when you start to sweat. And for the record, it's remarkably easy to push your buttons and make that happen." She also closed her laptop, then stood and started to do her stretching.

Cal forced his gaze away from the seductive sight and held in a groan. Just like that he did, in fact, start to sweat, proving that Miss Prim and Proper was right about him being easy. But no way was she right about close proximity turning a man and woman into a couple. The only couple he recognized was him and work.

And Justine worked for him. No matter how beautiful and intriguing she happened to be, he was her boss. Sure, he'd been preoccupied with her. But he broke his leg—there was nothing wrong with his eyesight. Noticing that a woman was pretty, shapely and sexy was hardwired into him. But he knew where the line was drawn. His R-rated thoughts would be an issue only if he crossed it. He'd had a chance to fire her and wasn't sure whether or not he was sorry he hadn't.

"We haven't finished discussing the list of activities I came up with for you." Her statement came out of the blue.

"What?"

"Yesterday you challenged me to come up with a list of things someone in a cast could participate in. Without a wheelchair. Remember?"

"Vividly. Especially the part where you tried to abandon me on the beach."

"You're so dramatic."

"And you want to discuss it in more detail," he guessed.

"Actually, no. Because that would be your cue to push back and find something wrong with each and every one of them."

"You're implying that I don't have an open mind?" he accused her.

"Implying is too vague. I'm flat-out saying that you refuse to even consider any leisure interest in which your safety wouldn't be jeopardized. And no one who has a lick of sense would let a man with a cast on his leg go wave riding. Which leaves the matter of alternatives."

He smiled because she had him dead to rights. "You must have me mixed up with the vacation Grinch."

"My mistake." There was a knock on the door and she said, "That must be lunch."

Sometime in the week that she'd been here, Cal had let her take over deciding on the menu, and so far her choices had been perfect. Also, sometime since her splashdown in his life, annoyance at the work interruption had turned into anticipation at the prospect of sharing the meal with her and wondering what she would say next.

The room service waiters set up everything at the dining room table and Justine signed the check. With the ever-popular let-us-know-if-you-need-further-assistance, they quietly left the villa. Cal crutched himself over and sat down.

"Smells good," he said, realizing he was hungry.

"I hope you like it. I was assured that this is a signature dish for the chef."

He lifted the silver dome over his plate and the smells got even better. "Sea bass."

"Yup. Along with risotto, salad and vegetables sautéed in olive oil."

"One of my favorites."

"Mine, too." She sat in her usual place at a right angle to him.

They ate in silence for a few moments, savoring the delicate flavors, the way they all complemented each other. Watching her enjoy her food was about the sexiest thing he'd ever seen. He had to say something before he swallowed his tongue.

He glanced at the other things on the table and wondered if she'd missed something. "What, no dessert?"

"About that—" She met his gaze. "You're going to have it later."

"Am I?"

"Absolutely, because I know how important it is to you. I've been asking around, and—"

He had an uneasy feeling. "Where am I going?"

"It's a surprise." She was looking very mysterious, which was the opposite of comforting.

"Does it have anything to do with that list of things for a mobility-challenged person to do without a wheelchair?"

"As a matter of fact—" she chewed the last bite of sea bass and swallowed "—the list is now a spreadsheet. Your idea."

He wished he'd never confessed about the bet and his strategy for dealing with it. "You didn't."

"It's morphed into a schedule. Something different every day. Not unlike what you had planned before your unfortunate accident."

"What if I don't want to be that scheduled?"

"Let's ignore the fact that you sound like a disgruntled eleven-year-old. Look at it as an opportunity to silence your guilty conscience, stay true to the spirit of the bet and learn how to do down time. In the process you'll feel really good about yourself."

"Okay. None of that is going to happen. And before you accuse me of pushing back and finding something wrong for no reason, this is for the sake of argument. What are we doing this afternoon?"

"I'm not—"

"Yes, you are. I'm not going alone. So, give it to me straight."

"It's a surprise." She wiped her mouth with the cloth napkin, then set it by her plate.

The only surprise he was in favor of was her walking into the room naked. Zero chance of that happening, so he said, "If you won't reveal the secret activity, it means I'm not going to like the surprise."

Her look challenged him. "Let's go and find out."

"I thought participating in activities was supposed to relax a person."

Justine ignored the death-by-stare look Cal gave her and threaded another reed into the beginner basket she was weaving. "Are you whining? Because that sounded an awful lot like a whine to me."

"Is that any way to talk to your boss?"

"It's the same way I've talked to you since I arrived. Seems a little late to start complaining about it now." She looked up at him sitting beside her on the bench at the picnic table. They were in a group craft lesson where she was trying to ignore the heat that consumed her every time Cal's shoulder or any other part of him touched her.

"There are limits to what I'll endure," he grumbled.

"Probably. But so far I haven't seen it. Makes me feel powerful."

"Good for you." He glared down at the mess of split, torn and discarded reeds in front of him. "For the record, I was right."

"Of course you'd think that." She pushed her threaded fronds closer together to make the weave tighter. "But because I'm a good assistant and kindhearted, too, I'll humor you. What is it you think you're right about?"

"That statement, Miss Walker, is the very definition

of patronizing, and if I'm not mistaken, there was a good deal of condescension thrown in, too."

"Excellent that you noticed." She smiled up at him. "I was afraid you'd missed it."

His lips twitched, canceling out his bad-tempered remarks. "What I'm right about is that you surprised me with a basket weaving class precisely because you knew I would hate it."

"Your open-mindedness is truly inspiring."

"Don't think that sunny attitude will distract me." There was a twinkle in his eyes. "Everyone knows basket weaving is a joke. It's what you tell your parents your college major is in order to watch their hair turn white."

She laughed. "On the contrary. It's big business. There are classes all over the States and supply stores. Serious stuff. These baskets can be decorative or practical."

He looked ruefully at his attempt. "Not from where I'm sitting."

"Cheer up, Cal. Don't forget I promised you ice cream afterward if you're a good boy. That's why I didn't order dessert at lunch. It's part of the surprise."

He ripped another reed trying to get it into place and swore under his breath. "Tell me again how this is supposed to be relaxing."

"Because you're not being graded."

"Ha." He gestured to the eight or ten people working at other tables. "They're all judging and not in a happy way. I can feel it."

She looked around and in spite of his complaints, this class delivered on its promise—beginning basket weaving in paradise. She'd found it online, offered at a nearby resort, signed them up and arranged transportation. The tables were in an open-sided structure and shaded by a thatched roof. There was a spectacular view of the ocean, and flowered shrubs, palm trees and grass surrounded them. A sea breeze made the air temperature practically perfect.

"Let me explain the concept of vacation to you." She picked up another reed and easily worked it through while teaching her boss the intricacies of Vacation 101. "Most of your time is spent doing things that are important for one reason or another. Making money, sustaining jobs, providing a service or product. The prospect of not being able to fulfill one of those commitments produces stress."

"I'm painfully aware of all that—"

"And I'm aware that you're aware." She held up a hand to stop him when he opened his mouth to argue. "It's vacation you're woefully inadequate with. The stress will burn you out if you don't take a break and figure out how to power down. It's a time when you can do nothing at all." She held up her basket. "Or do something that doesn't matter whether or not you succeed."

"It matters to me."

"You're a perfectionist." She nodded her understanding. "That's a completely different motivational speech and I don't have the notes with me."

He looked unhappily at the mess of destroyed foliage in front of him. "I don't like wasting anything—resources or time. Since I have nothing to show for this hour, it must be classified as wasteful."

Justine watched his determined attempt to weave another reed into his creation. His big hands were not delicate, making the task harder. On top of that he was all thumbs. Athleticism didn't automatically translate to an activity requiring fine motor skills. And yet she thought he was completely adorable. A fish out of water who made her insides tap dance. Words that she would never say out loud.

"Okay, tell me this. In the last hour have you thought about work even once?"

His big hands stilled as he considered the question. "No."

She grinned at him. "Mission accomplished."

"Not really." He glanced at the people who were standing up now, showing off their beginner baskets before drifting off to their next recreational pursuit.

"Did you see that?" Cal met her gaze. "Everyone else made a functional item. A receptacle capable of holding something. Post-its. Paper clips or staples."

"Vacation means you have to stop looking at the world through a prism of work. What those people made could be used to hold individual eye shadows, seasoning packets or hair accessories."

"Exactly. They made something useful." He held up his sad attempt. "This is a flat nothing."

"Well, you really are Danny Downer today." She tapped her lip, mulling over the misshapen thing. "Maybe it could be a place mat."

"For a rodent." He shifted, moving his injured leg to a more comfortable position.

"Oh, please…" She took a breath and counted, taking control of the shivers skipping through her when his arm brushed hers. Studying the irregular square, she said, "I see the beginning of an area rug."

"Seriously?" He gave her an incredulous look.

"Why not? The journey of a thousand miles starts with a single step."

"It must be exhausting," he said.

"What?"

"Being a glass-half-full person all the time." He shook his head.

There was a time when she wasn't. Her heart caught

as memories kaleidoscoped through her mind—a man's strong arm draped casually across her shoulders, a laughing, red-haired toddler. But when a person suddenly lost their spouse, child and reason for living, the line between despair and optimism was razor-thin. She'd walked it a long, painful time, more than once nearly slipping into the emptiness.

Then she made a choice, a conscious decision to focus on the positive. At first it was impossible to find anything hopeful. But she found if you worked on something long enough it became a habit. Still, she could never forget that the habit had grown out of the glass-half-empty time of her life.

Working those optimism muscles now, she managed to smile at him. "How about that ice cream?"

"If it means I don't have to work with these weeds anymore, I'll race you," he said.

She laughed. "I wouldn't want to take advantage of a man on crutches."

"My odds are improving." He stood, balancing on his uninjured leg while he reached for the crutches leaning against the end of the table beside him. "I'm getting pretty fast on these things."

"No argument there." She got to her feet and picked up the woven basket she'd made. He, on the other hand, was walking away without his. "Aren't you going to take yours?"

"My what?" He pivoted and met her gaze. "It isn't anything."

"Sure it is."

"What?" There was still faux bitterness in his voice.

"Maybe a coaster?"

He rolled his eyes. "If you leave it I'll buy the ice cream."

"No way. This is my treat."

The little shop was located down a path right near the hotel's lobby. It was a charming place with circular tables and metal chairs that had padded red seats and heart-shaped backs. Behind the glass display case, the different flavors of ice cream were displayed.

The young woman behind the counter was wearing a white apron and a big smile. "What can I get you?"

"I'd like a scoop of cookies-and-cream. In a dish, please," Justine said.

"A decisive woman," Cal observed. "Remarkable."

"And for you, sir?"

"Make mine two scoops of salted caramel vanilla with chocolate sauce." He looked down. "The second one is my reward for persevering today."

"I'm not judging," she assured him.

"Both good choices," the ice-cream lady said. "I'll have it ready in a jiffy."

Cal insisted on buying, and Justine was both pleased and uncomfortable. Even though he expensed her presence here for work-related items on the island, his buying even a simple thing like ice cream had a more intimate vibe. It seemed personal and she didn't know what to do with that. She carried their cups to a corner table because he had his hands full of crutches. When they were settled, both of them started eating. Did he feel awkward or was it just her? Not a question she was going to ask.

After a few moments of silence, Cal said, "This is really good. Almost worth the humiliation of that class."

"I think you secretly enjoyed it. Or maybe the part you liked best was picking on me and complaining. Of course you'd never admit it if I'm right."

"About that…"

"So I am right," she said triumphantly.

"No. I really hated it." He met her gaze and his expression turned serious. "But I was taking it out on you. Did I say something wrong?"

"No." That answer was automatic because she had no idea what he was talking about. Then curiosity kicked in. "When? What? I'm not sure what you mean."

"When I asked if it makes you tired being upbeat all the time. You had a funny look on your face. And by funny, I mean sad."

Bam. There was her reminder that he didn't miss a detail. And didn't forget. After his question, she'd been thinking about pulling herself out of the dark pit of depression she'd fallen into following an unimaginable loss. It was quite extraordinary that after their stroll for ice cream and ordering it, he would remember her reaction to his offhand remark.

"I hope you know I was teasing," he said sincerely.

"Yes."

"What were you thinking about?" he asked.

"Stuff." Not an ice-cream sundae conversation. "And it's only fair to warn you that I have a dark side."

As she'd hoped, he interpreted her remark as more teasing. "You have layers. That just makes you more interesting."

"I'm a lot like basket weaving." The look on his face made her laugh. "What you saw on my face was empathy for the poor palm fronds who were sad. Many reeds were sacrificed in the artistic yet noble pursuit of your trivet."

"There it is." He pointed his spoon at her. "The snarky streak is strong in you."

"May it live long and prosper," she joked.

"Unlike my weaving skills."

"The only way to improve is by doing. Practice and repetition."

"Please don't make me."

The serious mood scattered, replaced by teasing and banter. Just the way she liked it. Because thinking about Cal made her head hurt. He had so many wonderful qualities and today she'd discovered another one. Two, actually. He was perceptive and sensitive. If she had known how much she would like this man, all the money in the world wouldn't have made her take this job.

Chapter Seven

Cal was more than happy to shoot his mouth off when he was right but not so much when Justine was. Especially since he'd given her such a hard time about non-work activities. The truth was, he'd had a great time on the outing this afternoon. Oh, he did in fact loathe basket weaving, but it was fun finding out that he shouldn't quit his day job for it.

On top of that, the break from work had been rejuvenating. Considering all of that, a different setting for dinner seemed like an excellent idea. With Justine, of course.

He saw her pick up the phone at her desk and knew what was coming. "Are you planning to order room service?"

"Yes." She set the receiver down again. "Was there something in particular you wanted?"

"There is, actually. I'd like to try the five-star restaurant here at the resort."

"Oh?" She smiled and there was a little smugness in it. "Someone had a good time today and is looking to broaden his horizons again."

So much for thinking she might not notice there was a connection. "Okay. The field trip didn't bite. You've got thirty seconds for a victory lap and then we're moving on."

"Only thirty seconds?"

He looked at his watch. "And…go."

"Am I allowed to say I told you so?"

"At your own peril," he warned her.

"Okay. I told you so." She grinned, a look full of satisfaction, and damned if it didn't look good on her. "Whatever peril you have planned is worth it."

"Good, because you're going with me to try that five-star restaurant."

"Oh—" The smile disappeared. "I'm not sure—"

"No you don't. You're not wiggling out of this. I want to go to the restaurant, and better than anyone you know how resistant I've been to outings. That suggests I'm going a little stir-crazy. You must be, too, eating here all the time. There's just one condition."

"What's that?" she asked suspiciously.

"When you're back to work in Blackwater Lake, tell everyone what a sweetheart of a boss I am."

Justine laughed, a lovely, happy sound. "So the next time you break your leg on vacation, everyone will volunteer for drudge duty on a tropical island paradise?"

"And I thought I was being so subtle." He got up from the sofa and propped himself on the crutches, then moved over to the desk. "Don't make me eat alone."

"Well…it would be nice to get out of the villa." She glanced around the elegantly appointed deluxe surroundings and laughed. "Now, there's something I never expected to say."

"Excellent."

"I'll make a reservation."

An hour later the resort's golf cart shuttle dropped them off in front of a stand-alone building adjacent to the hotel's main five-story tower. Out front there was lush landscaping, including flowers in yellow, red and pink. Tiki torches lighted the path to the heavy front doors with vertical handles.

Cal was going to be a gentleman if it killed him. He hobbled over and balanced himself on his one good leg, then opened the door. "After you."

"I could have done that," she scolded him. "You don't have to show off for the hired help."

It hit him that he *was* showing off and didn't think of her as only an employee. His perception had changed and he wasn't exactly sure when that happened. When she'd demonstrated her stretching moves? Or the day she'd half carried him to that lounge on the beach and he got just a taste of her appealing curves? Maybe it happened today when the basket weaving and ice cream had turned into a flirt fest. At least, he thought she'd been flirting and knew for a fact he had been.

No one would accuse him of understanding how a woman's mind worked, but he wasn't entirely clueless, either. A little rusty, but not oblivious. They'd had fun together today. Not that work couldn't be fun, too, but it was different outside the office, even if his office was in a luxury villa. He decided to let the showing off remark pass without a comment. Anything he said would just complicate an already complicated thing.

"Chivalry is not dead." Holding the door open with his shoulder, he breathed in the floral scent of her skin as she walked past him.

There was a high desk, and an attractive woman who must be the hostess stood behind it, waiting. She gave them a friendly smile to go along with the greeting. "Good evening, Mr. Hart. I do hope your leg is mending nicely."

"Feeling much better, thanks. I'll be in a walking cast soon."

"That's good to hear. I have a lovely, secluded table for two. The most romantic we have, in my opinion."

His assistant opened her mouth, probably to clarify that this wasn't a romantic dinner. Before she could get the words out he said, "Lead the way. I'll follow you, Justine."

She hesitated a moment and there was a confused expression on her face. Then she shrugged and said, "Okay."

Several couples dined at nearby tables and watched curiously as they passed. A few minutes later they were sitting at a booth in the corner. There was a pristine white tablecloth and a lighted candle along with fresh flowers in the center of it. And silver salt and pepper shakers.

"Lorenzo will be your waiter," the hostess informed them. "You're in good hands with him."

"Thanks," Cal said.

Justine looked around and said, "This is nice."

"Yeah."

There was elegant dark wood trim on the walls and paintings of the ocean and local landscape. It was quiet except for the low hum of voices. Moments after they settled, their waiter appeared.

"My name is Lorenzo and it's my pleasure to take care of such a beautiful young couple."

Justine lifted a finger, signaling her intention of setting him straight. "You should know—"

"When did you arrive on our beautiful island?" the middle-aged man asked.

"About a week ago," she answered. "And I have to tell you that—"

"You're going to tell me that you're honeymooners. I suspected since this is your first visit to Castaways Restaurant. I would remember if you had been here before. But you've been keeping to yourselves. Being alone is the goal of a honeymoon, but sooner or later a change of scenery is good—to keep the romance alive. Yes?"

"It's a challenge." Justine's tone was wry. Apparently she'd decided not to burst the guy's bubble. "Especially with a broken leg."

Lorenzo made a sympathetic *tsk*ing sound. "A story from your honeymoon trip to share and laugh about one day."

"Right." Cal noticed empathetic looks from other male diners around them.

"It is my job to make sure you keep up your strength. For healing." He winked as he handed over the menus. "Can I get you something from the bar?"

"Wine?" Cal looked at his assistant, who shrugged as if to say, *Why not?*

"I'd like a list, please."

"Of course, sir." The waiter left and moments later returned to hand it over.

Cal studied the choices and saw one of his favorite labels, an expensive and very nice pinot noir. Justine confirmed that red was fine with her and he ordered a bottle. Lorenzo disappeared and they were alone again.

"So," she said, "that guy is full of local color."

"And observant," Cal joked. "Pegging us as being on our honeymoon."

"I know, right?" She laughed.

"Congratulations." The middle-aged man sitting at the table closest to them raised a wineglass. His companion had just left, presumably to visit the ladies' room. "I couldn't help overhearing."

Cal wasn't sure how to respond. She was his assistant and they were working together, but that explanation would get a wink and a *Yeah, right, that's what they all say.* Whether or not they ever saw this guy again, Cal wouldn't take a chance that Justine might be embarrassed. So he shrugged and let the man believe what he wanted.

"Tough break," their table neighbor said, glancing at the cast up to the knee. "The leg, I mean. Don't let it hold you back, if you know what I mean."

"I'm pretty sure we do," Justine said wryly. "Thanks for the advice."

"My wife and I are celebrating ten years together. This is our anniversary trip. The kids are with my folks."

"Congratulations," Cal said. "What's the secret to marital longevity?"

"Listening," he answered promptly.

"Excuse me?"

"It's a component of communication. We took a marriage seminar because I interrupted all the time and it was driving Carol nuts." He shrugged. "Turns out if you're thinking about what you're going to say next, you're not really listening to what she's saying."

"Makes sense," Cal told him.

"Seems simple, right?" The guy laughed. "It takes a lot of practice but it's worth the effort. And the other thing I would say is to make the most of alone time. Before you know it, kids come along and it's not just the two of you anymore. I'm not knocking it. I love my kids, and having a family is the best thing that ever happened to me. It's just that you have to work a little harder on the couple thing. Don't take it for granted."

Cal was looking at Justine and noticed a wistful expression on her face. That seemed to happen when the subject of couples and kids came up. "I can see how that happens."

"So," the stranger said, "this is worth what you paid

for it, but look at that cast not as an obstacle but as an opportunity."

His wife returned to the table and gave him a look. "Alan?"

"What? Just chatting up the honeymoon couple and sharing what's worked for us, sweetie." He did seem sincere. "It's been the best ten years of my life."

"Congratulations on your anniversary," Justine said.

"Thank you." Carol sat down. "I hope the two of you will be as happy as we've been."

Lorenzo returned with a bottle and two glasses, and they went through the ritual of checking the label, tasting and pouring. Cal stole looks at Justine and saw her stealing looks at the other couple. There was such longing on her face mixed with a generous dose of envy.

The more time he spent with her, the more intrigued he became. She'd obviously wanted to correct the erroneous impression of them as honeymooners, then had gone along with it. That took Cal to a place where he wondered what it would be like if they were a couple. The thoughts seemed to throw kerosene on the sparks of his fascination with her body and all that he hadn't seen.

He wanted to know more about her. Was she flirting earlier today? Could she be as attracted to him as he was to her? Unless he was way off the mark, that was very possible, and he didn't think he was so rusty that he was seeing things that weren't there.

That decided, he planned to test his theory.

Justine and Cal stood outside the restaurant, waiting for the shuttle to pick them up for the return trip to the villa. It was a night so beautiful, she had no words to describe the spectacular dusting of stars glittering in the sky. A nearly full moon bathed them in silver light and a gentle breeze brushed strands of hair back from her face. Sharing a bottle of wine meant she'd had two glasses and that was a lot for her, but this happy haze was really nice.

"You're very quiet," Cal observed. "Did the whole mistaken honeymooner thing upset you?"

"No. It obviously made Lorenzo and Mr. and Mrs. Ten-Year Anniversary happy to think that we were. I finally decided that setting everyone straight would somehow let them down. No harm done." She sighed. "It was perfect. In fact, this whole day has been absolutely perfect."

"Even the work part?"

"It's necessary and made me appreciate the rest of the day. Balance. Don't you agree?"

"It was great, with the exception of the basket weaving class, where I was a standout underachiever."

"That should have made you appreciate having ice cream afterward, a wonderful dinner and the excellence of this moment right now." She breathed deeply. "Smell the flowers mixed with the sea air. It's simply…paradise."

The golf cart shuttle pulled up in front of them just then, cutting off his answer, but she dared him to disagree. Justine climbed in and slid over to make room for Cal. He handled the maneuver so gracefully she almost forgot he was on crutches. When they were safely in, Cal instructed the driver where to drop them, and the guy took off.

The movement was so sudden that she lurched forward. Automatically Cal put his arm around her shoulders, settling her securely against him. He was strong and solid, the kind of man a woman could depend on. She prepared herself for him to let her go when the ride smoothed out, but he didn't. And she wasn't sure what to make of that.

Feeling their bodies pressed together was more intoxicating than the lush, lovely night. The inclination to lean her head on his shoulder was strong, and if the ride had lasted any longer she almost certainly would have succumbed to temptation. But before she was ready for it to end, the driver pulled to a stop in front of the path lined with bushes and trees that protected the villa's privacy.

Cal tipped the driver, and it must have been generous because the man thanked him profusely. They slid out and stepped safely back from the vehicle before watching it dart forward. Then solitude surrounded them along with the moonlight. She had had such a good time and felt oddly like Cinderella at the ball when it was five minutes until the clock struck midnight. Five minutes to soak up the magic before the world turned back into ordinary.

"I think you should have moved the Hart Energy corporate offices to this island," she said.

"An interesting thought." There was a smile in his voice. "I wonder if anyone would move here and work for me."

"When I get back to Blackwater Lake and sing your praises, that won't be an issue for you ever again," she vowed.

"Okay. That makes me feel obligated to reveal that the secret to keeping me in line is setting parameters."

"Better known as laying down the law," she said.

"Yes." He was studying her closely. "So, you're not sorry you came?"

"Absolutely not."

He angled his head toward the villa's front door. "Then can I interest you in a nightcap?"

"I'd like that very much." It's what Cinderella would have done if her fairy godmother had given her even the slightest bit of wiggle room on that deadline. "On one condition."

"Which is?"

"We can sit on the patio and enjoy this night. When we go home, winter and the holidays will be staring us in the face. Let's take advantage of this setting while we can."

"I don't know. You drive a pretty hard bargain. Let me think about it." A moment later he said, "I thought about it and you're on."

They went inside and Cal leaned on the crutches while he poured brandy into two snifters. "Will you do me a favor and carry—"

"Happy to take them outside." She'd thought ahead, knowing he'd have his hands full with the crutches.

With glasses in hand, Justine followed him through the French doors onto the patio. Pool and patio lights were on, illuminating the area with two chairs and a small table between them. When Cal was settled, she set down his drink, then sat on his right, a couple of feet away.

Not quite near enough to feel the heat from his body. Her heart skipped and she missed the closeness they'd shared in the golf cart shuttle. Since he was her boss, that probably should have been a red flag, warning of trouble. But, since she was identifying with female characters from books tonight, she was going to channel Scarlett O'Hara and worry about it tomorrow.

"That was the best dinner I've ever had in my life," she gushed.

"It was good," he agreed.

She noticed the tone and glanced at him. There was something in his expression that made her ask, "You've had better?"

"My meal tonight was excellent. And the companionship was exceptional." There was a gleam in his eyes.

"No you don't." She wagged a finger at him. "It's not going to work. I refuse to be distracted. Where have you ever had a better dining experience than we had tonight at the five-star restaurant on this island?"

"It's a very close call, but I'd have to go with Paris."

"Oh. Well. Paris." She shrugged. "I guess that's to be expected. Do you remember the name of the restaurant?"

The corners of his mouth curved up. "No, but I'm pretty sure it was French."

She laughed. "Only in Paris would they give a restaurant a French name."

"Go figure." He sipped his brandy.

"In the City of Light, do the waiters automatically assume a couple dining alone together are honeymooners?"

"I couldn't say about all of them. But in my case, I was on my honeymoon."

"Oh?"

"Yes, I took Daria—Tate, of the Dallas Tates—to Europe for our honeymoon. I combined the trip with business to research alternative energy sources. They're doing some remarkable work with algae."

"Oh, be still my heart. You got a tax deduction for taking your bride to Paris after your wedding? Oh, Cal—" She groaned, then couldn't help laughing. "And everyone wondered why the marriage didn't work out."

"I couldn't be objective then, but now it's clear to me what the problem was."

"That there was no romance?" She found herself deeply curious about his relationship. More than she should be, given that they were boss and assistant.

"If she hadn't fallen in love with my brother first, then made me her rebound guy, a trip to energy-rich land in the middle of nowhere would have been fun." He looked at her, intensity crackling in his eyes. "With the right woman, anywhere would have been romantic."

"You're right."

"I am?"

The shocked expression on his face was so darn cute it made her laugh. "Did you want me to disagree?"

"Of course not. But I expected some pushback."

"Sorry to disappoint."

"You are surprising and many other things, but disappointing is not one of them."

Justine didn't know whether to be flattered or ask for a raise. Since he was already paying her very generously, asking for more seemed wrong. "I agree with you because it makes sense. It's practical. The feelings come from within and you take them wherever you go. The place doesn't have to be special if you're with the right person."

"Well said. And it begs the question—did you have a honeymoon?"

Although she didn't want to talk about this, it wasn't fair to grill him like raw hamburger, then refuse to answer his question. If anything, she was unsure why he hadn't brought this up before now. She took a sip of her brandy and let it burn all the way to her belly.

"Sort of."

He waited a few moments, probably giving her a chance to elaborate. When she didn't, he asked, "What does that mean?"

She took a deep breath and counted to five, willing herself to relax. "We had no money and were too poor to go anywhere."

"That doesn't explain the 'sort of.'"

"No, it doesn't. And I heard the pity in your voice in case you were wondering. There's no reason for it. Our 'honeymoon' was the best."

"What did you do?" He cleared his throat. "I mean, I know *what* you did. But something made it the best. Tell me about that."

"My husband was planning to paint our apartment anyway, so he drew a picture of a fireplace on one wall." She smiled, remembering how young they'd been and how wonderful it was. "It was August in Dallas and there was a heat wave. The humidity was awful. But we made a bed on the floor in front of that fireplace art and pretended we were snowed in at a cabin. It was sweet and romantic and just right. We didn't have two pennies to rub together but felt like we had everything a person could ever want."

"You're lucky. I was in Paris and we were barely speaking to each other."

"I'm sorry, Cal."

He shrugged. "It's in the past. Putting a positive spin on the whole thing, it was a learning experience."

"Now who's being a glass-half-full person? And yet, it's kind of sad."

"Not anymore." He met her gaze, and his turned thoughtful. "But I can't help wondering—"

"About?"

"What happened?"

"We turned up the air-conditioning and snuggled together for the whole weekend. Both of us had to go back to work on Monday."

"No." He shook his head. "That's not what I was asking. When you asked if I was married, I said no, and the next question was whether or not there was a divorce."

"I remember." She tensed, knowing what was coming.

"When I said there had been a divorce, you wanted to know what broke us up." He took a breath. "When I asked if you were married, you answered in the past tense but never talked about a divorce. What happened to your husband, Justine?"

Chapter Eight

Cal forgot about the moon, stars, perfect night and romance. He was mesmerized by her body language. It went from lush and loose to tight and tense in a heartbeat. Part of him wished he could take back the question, but another part wanted to know everything about this woman. She was special and whatever she'd gone through had contributed to the person who sat to his right. She was close enough for him to feel the warmth of her skin and hear the slight increase in her breathing.

What she'd already told him was that a car accident had left her with a limp that mostly she was able to hide. But he had a bad feeling her husband was tragically connected to the accident.

Justine was quiet for a long moment, staring at her empty brandy snifter. He wanted to pull her into his arms so badly that it hurt, but all he could do was wait and hope she would share whatever was making her look like that.

In the end he couldn't stand the silence and gently nudged her to answer. "Justine? What is it?"

She looked up at him then. "My husband, Wes, died in a car accident along with our little girl, Betsy. It wasn't his fault and she wasn't even two yet."

Cal felt as if she'd just slugged him in the stomach with a two-by-four. He'd put the pieces together with her husband but didn't know she'd had a child. He thought of his niece, who was just a little older than Betsy was when she'd died, and what losing Leah would do to his sister, Ellie. Devastating didn't even describe it. He couldn't think of words adequate to express such a loss.

"My, God—I—" He'd been about to say how sorry he was, but that sounded so stupid.

"It's all right. You don't have to say anything."

"I do. But anything I can think of sounds trite and inconsequential."

"Don't worry about it, Cal."

What was wrong with this picture? Her comforting him? "No, just give me a minute. I'll come up with something besides 'I'm sorry.'"

"Believe it or not, that happened a lot. People want to make you feel better and that's the accepted phrasing, with slight variations." She smiled sadly. "It made me so furious at first, because no one could possibly be sorrier than me."

"It's a helpless feeling," he admitted, "not having something to say besides 'That really sucks.' Not a comfortable place to be."

"In hindsight I appreciated that friends and family were there for me. But at the time, the anger inside me was so big, so consuming. I was looking for someone to blame, a target for my rage. But there wasn't one."

"What about the other driver? The one who caused the accident?"

She set her glass on the table between them, then folded her hands in her lap. "He was an older man who'd had a medical episode—heart attack or stroke. He lost control at the wheel and plowed his big, heavy car into ours. The impact was on the driver's side and Betsy was strapped into her seat behind her daddy. So I could see her from the front passenger seat."

Cal swore he heard a break in her voice, but she looked composed. There was no sheen of tears in her eyes. This time he had to say something—even if it was clichéd and stupid. "You know, playing 'what if' or 'if only' will make you crazy, right?"

"You mean what if she'd been behind my seat? Or if only she wasn't in the car at all?" She met his gaze. "Yeah, I know. For a long time I lived in 'if only'-ville. While there I met my three BFFs—'what if,' 'you should have,' and 'why didn't you.'"

"Sounds like an inhospitable place," he commented.

"It is. I don't recommend visiting."

"Not high on my list."

"The problem was that I had a lot of time on my hands in the hospital."

"The accident. That's how you got the limp." Duh. She'd told him that very first day when she arrived on the island to work. It seemed more pronounced after her long flight, and in the days since, he'd noticed that when she was tired or needed to stretch it was the most obvious.

"What caused the limp?"

"My leg was shattered from the knee down." Her voice was calm and controlled, as if talking about a glass she'd dropped on the floor. "For a while, the doctors thought I might lose it. They fought for me because there was a time when I really didn't care one way or the other. I was damaged in places the doctors couldn't fix, parts of me hurt so much more than my leg."

"Survivor's guilt," he commented.

"Yes." Absently she brushed a hand over her thigh. "For the longest time I tried to understand. Why didn't

I die, too? What made me so special that my life was spared? Was I saved for some divine purpose?" Her expression was wry. "I didn't get any answers to those questions and it was very frustrating, I can tell you."

"I can't even imagine." Cal could see that she'd loved her family very much, and he had no frame of reference. Except... "The idea of suddenly losing my parents, my brothers or sister, my niece... It's unthinkable. How does a person get through that? How did you move from such a dark place?" To the strong, sassy, serene woman he knew now. And he had to ask, "What's your secret?"

"To what?" She met his gaze.

"You obviously pulled yourself out of the pit of hell. You're tough, smart, efficient and a really good assistant. Shanna is better, but that's because we've worked together for a number of years. Still, you're a close second. No matter how much no one wanted to work with me, the fact is that Human Resources wouldn't have sent someone incompetent." So he looked into her eyes and tried not to drown in the beauty, warmth and sadness. "How did you come back from the edge?"

"Yoga."

"There has to be more." He'd seen her stretching and breathing and she'd instructed him on the technique for relaxation. But it just couldn't be that easy.

She shrugged. "I was in the hospital a long time and had multiple surgeries to save my leg. When the docs gave me the green light for exercise, I had rehabilitation and physical therapy. That's where I found yoga's healing for mind, body and spirit. It changed my life."

And watching her yoga poses had changed his, Cal thought. Although that carnal reflection didn't make him proud. And for a moment he was afraid he'd actually said it out loud, but when the placid expression on her face didn't change, he figured he was in the clear.

"You are a remarkable woman, Justine Walker."

That was the truth and he hadn't meant it in an intimate way, just a statement of fact. But when the words were out of his mouth, they felt very personal. He felt personal. His gaze wandered to the pool and its lights under the crystal clear water. He remembered Justine swimming in the dark, staying in the water while talking to him, then pretending to hear his cell phone ring so she could get out and put on a cover-up. Clearly she didn't want him to see her from the waist down, and it dawned on him that her self-consciousness was also tied to the accident. It was why she always wore long pants and dresses that fell to the floor.

"Your leg is scarred, isn't it?"

"Yes," she said without hesitation. "Surgery is an invasive technique to fix the body, but you have to inflict trauma on the outside in order to repair what's wrong underneath. A catch-22 for doctors who have taken an oath to do no harm."

She looked at him for a moment, conflict raging in her eyes, then seemed to make a decision. Slowly she slid the hem of her dress to just above her knee. Thick, purplish-red marks marred the skin and crisscrossed her shin and calf.

"There were a lot of surgeries," she said simply.

He nodded. "I can't believe how much I whined about something as insignificant as a broken leg. I'm officially a candy ass."

She laughed. "If anyone knows how much a broken leg hurts, it's me."

"Still, the least I could have done is bite down on a stick and set it myself."

There was amusement in her eyes when she said, "Have I ever told you you're very dramatic?"

"Probably. But I'm cured now."

"Hardly. It's in your nature, I think." She let her skirt fall and cover the scarring that clearly made her ill at ease.

Cal had a nature, all right, but he wouldn't call it dramatic. Dishonorable, distasteful, detestable and sleazy would certainly describe his nature. The disfigurement she'd revealed to him was both deep and shocking, but the sight of it did not take the edge off his wanting her. And that was damned inconvenient.

It was tangible proof of the profound loss she'd experienced with the death of her husband and child. Continuing to want her was bad enough, but hitting on her in spite of it would make him the slimiest life form on the planet. He was a guy and couldn't help the attraction that wouldn't go away, but there were lines a decent man wouldn't cross. Cal considered himself a decent man, and this was one of those uncrossable lines.

"I just got this report faxed from the corporate office." Justine sat on the couch beside her boss. She was ready to take notes as he looked it over. It was the way he liked to work. "Ready when you are."

"I'll look it over later and make notations in the margin." He put the papers on the coffee table, topping a stack that would eventually end up on her desk to deal with.

"Good. Because lunch will be here soon. You must be starving."

"Not really."

That was odd since he'd picked at his food that morning. He was a big man with a healthy appetite and missing a meal was out of character for him. "Are you feeling all right?"

"Fine. I guess my physical restrictions have pared down my need to eat."

Justine had been here almost two weeks and in that time saw no evidence of that until the last couple of days. It was official. Cal was acting weird, and not just in his eating habits. He was avoiding her—some with the work stuff, but mostly everything else. No field trips to weave reeds into something functional—or not.

The only difference was that she'd told him about losing her family. Maybe that cured him of wanting to talk to her. Or seeing her hideous scars had turned him off. Or worse. He pitied her. And that just made her insane. But since the night they'd gone to the restaurant and were mistaken for honeymooners, he'd been distant.

Justine didn't like it. "You're sure you don't want to scan that report? I can respond if you have any questions or need clarifications."

"No, I'll get to it later. Why don't you work on email?" he suggested.

That would put her at the desk and far away from him. She could do that. Without a word she stood and moved across the room, then sat down in front of her laptop. There wasn't much to look at and nothing pressing. The way he'd acted, you'd have thought lasting world peace depended on her taking care of this.

In the process of trying to read his mind, she stole peeks at her boss and had been all morning. If she was being honest, she'd been doing that since the first day she came to work for him. Nine times out of ten she caught him looking back at her and the expression in his eyes made her pulse jump and her heart race. Not today. For all the notice he took of her, she could be a mixed green salad.

Mercifully there was a knock on the door, breaking the tension in the room.

"I'll get it." The words were automatic since she always took care of this.

Justine jumped up and hurried to let in the room service waiters. She'd gotten to know them pretty well and smiled at the two men. They were wearing their resort uniforms of dark slacks and beige cotton island-print shirts.

"Hi, William." She looked at the other man. "George, how is your little boy's cold? Is he feeling better?"

"Yes, ma'am." The dark-skinned, brown-eyed young man smiled. "He is getting into everything again."

"That's a good sign." She glanced at the other server. "William, did you patch things up with your girlfriend?"

"I took your advice, Miss Justine, and was honest with her about my feelings." His voice was heavily accented, like those of most of the staff who worked and lived on the island.

She walked with them to the dining table as they wheeled the cart over and set everything out. "And? How did it go?"

"She was very happy that I opened up and explained that talking about such things is not easy for me."

"A lot of men feel that way," she said sympathetically. "But we can't read your minds."

"So she told me. I asked for her patience and she was very understanding."

"I'm glad to hear that." At least she'd been useful to someone. She glanced over her shoulder at Cal, who was uncharacteristically engrossed in his laptop. "So, is the fish good today?"

George smiled. "It is perfection, Miss Justine."

"Great. You guys haven't steered me wrong yet." She

signed the room service check and the two waiters left with the wheeled cart. "Lunch is served."

Cal moved at the words, almost a flinch. Then his shoulders tensed. He stood and, without looking at her, said, "You go ahead. I'm not hungry."

"Really? You barely touched your breakfast." Then she wondered if he'd had a setback in his recovery. "Is your leg bothering you? Maybe we should call the doctor and—"

"I'm fine. Some air and sunshine are all I need."

"Then I'll help you get to the lounge. You can lean on me and—"

"No." The single word was almost as shocking as the loud crack of a bullet ricocheting around the room. He sighed, then turned toward her and said in a quiet, controlled voice, "I can make it by myself. You eat before the food gets cold."

And with that, he pivoted toward the exit and disappeared through the French doors. Justine crossed the room to watch and make sure he didn't fall. On the contrary, he made it easily, hopping on his good leg the two steps to where he stretched out in the shade of the palm trees. She could see only his legs, one muscular and tan, the other encased in white plaster.

Her feelings weren't hurt, exactly, that he hadn't insisted she keep him company. But she liked his wanting her around a lot better than shutting her out. And it wasn't so long ago that she'd tried very hard to avoid spending more time with her boss than was absolutely necessary.

Basket weaving and masquerading as honeymooners had certainly changed her attitude. This sudden cold shoulder was puzzling, to say the least.

"Be a jerk. See if I care," she said to herself. "You're not going to spoil my lunch."

She went back and plopped herself into one of the chairs at the dining table that suddenly seemed much too big. And a little bit lonely. A personality as big as Cal Hart's left a very large space to fill and Justine missed him. No one liked to eat alone but she'd been forced to get used to it. Until she took this job with Cal. This reaction was unexpected and, if she was being honest, a little disconcerting.

She lifted the silver dome from the plate and the perfect fish did look delicious, which was too bad. "Now I'm not hungry."

Her cell phone rang and she checked the display. She didn't recognize the number but answered anyway. Apparently it hadn't taken long for her to crave the sound of another human voice.

"Hello?"

"Miss Walker, this is Rudy from Island Tours. I'm double-checking your reservation for this afternoon, as you requested."

"Right." In case something work-related had unexpectedly come up, she wanted the company to be aware that a cancellation could happen. "Yes. We're still on." At least, she thought they were.

"Excellent. Then I'll see you and Mr. Hart at two o'clock."

"We'll be there." She crossed her fingers, hoping that wasn't a lie. It also meant she had to remind Cal. After basket weaving she ran all activities past him. No more surprises. He'd seemed enthusiastic about touring the island, but that was before.

Justine left the table and went outside. She walked past the patio table and pristine pool, then stopped to slip off her shoes before stepping into the sand. Uninvited and without a direct order, she sat in the lounge beside Cal's.

"It's good to see you relaxing." If this time-out in the sun had worked its magic and his normal attitude was restored, he would respond with something like *Do I look relaxed?* or *Relaxation is for sissies.*

"Yup. I am so calm."

Justine had seen tranquil and stress-free, and this wasn't it. He looked tense, tight and ready to snap any second. But she would play his little game. "Great. And there's more where this came from. We have a tour of the island this afternoon. An open-air jeep and knowledgeable driver will show us the high points and explain the history of this ocean paradise."

"Yeah, about that—"

"We discussed this and it's on your schedule," she reminded him.

His mouth pulled tight. "Something came up. I had to reschedule the conference call for this afternoon."

"I thought that was all arranged for tomorrow."

"The timing is delicate. It's about arranging financing for a project and everyone's available today."

As far as she'd known, everyone was on board for tomorrow, but she was nothing if not flexible. Even though she'd been looking forward to an afternoon drive along the ocean. But it would keep for another day.

"Okay," she said. "I'll call the tour company back and cancel."

"That's not necessary. You go."

By herself? "There's work. I'll need to be here to take notes during the call."

"I'll manage."

Was it her imagination or did he seem awfully eager to get rid of her?

"Take the afternoon off."

"Why?"

"Why what?" he asked.

"Why do you want me to take the afternoon off?"

"So you can go on the tour," he said. "It seems like canceling now is kind of abrupt."

"This is out of character for a man who thinks a fourteen-hour day is normal." She met his gaze. "And I made the reservation with the stipulation that there could be a sudden cancellation. Just in case something work-related came up. And it did."

"I'll be fine. You should go."

She studied the too eager, too sincere expression he was using to sell this idea. "Correct me if I'm wrong, but for the last conference call you insisted I be present, even though there was overtime involved." It was the only time since her first night, and it had been important.

"And I shouldn't have. So take this afternoon off. It's my way of making things up to you."

"What's really going on, Cal?"

He didn't answer right away, obviously thinking carefully about his response. "This is hard for me to admit, but it bothered me when you said no one wanted to work with me. I'm making a determined effort to change. So, take the time. I'm rehabilitating my image and I'd appreciate it if you'd help me out here, then spread the word back at the office about your excellent afternoon off."

Justine didn't buy this phony-baloney for a second. She'd scheduled the conference call with all parties involved and there was no conflict. The fact that Cal had been vague about details was a big clue that he was grasping at straws to get her out of here. And, presumably, to get out of spending the afternoon with her. If that's the way he wanted it…

"Okay." She stood. "It's a beautiful day for a drive. A real shame you have to miss it."

"Enjoy."

"I absolutely will," she said firmly.

And she wouldn't think about him.

Without another word she walked back to the villa. Her vow to put him out of her mind lasted less than a minute. The acute disappointment coursing through her meant something. Something big.

She was falling for Cal Hart. She refused to think the word *love*, but she was falling pretty deeply in like with the man. And wasn't that just her luck. She was finally ready to dip a toe back into the pool of life, only to be rejected by the man who had made her want to do it in the first place.

She had two more weeks with him and it was going to be hard. Trying to act as if she didn't notice his distant manner toward her that was in direct contrast to his attitude in the beginning was going to take everything she had.

Grit. That's what she needed. Fortunately she had a lot, earned the hard way. She'd never expected to use it on a man.

Chapter Nine

Vacation sucked.

Cal had experienced more stress since Justine Walker showed up than he had in four years of not taking time off. The guided tour of the island must have been good because she hadn't shown up for dinner, and he'd been surprised when it arrived since he hadn't thought to deal with food. Turned out her efficiency had no bounds, she'd ordered room service for one and everything was his favorite.

He wanted to be mad at her for abandoning him, but he'd given her the afternoon off and all but ordered her to take it. Selfishly it was to get a break from resisting the yearning to carry her to his bed and explore every inch of her bare skin. Although the carrying was a tad ambitious considering he was still on crutches, but when she was in the room some version of that fantasy never failed to roll through his mind.

Movement on the patio caught his attention, and he left the chair in his room where he was reading reports to hobble over to the open door. Justine stood there, straight and strong, the sole of one bare foot balanced against the other leg. She was wearing stretchy black pants that fit her like a second skin and a snug racerback top that sweetly outlined her breasts. She faced away from him and didn't know he was watching each successive gracefully executed pose.

Cal knew he was going to hell for not turning away but...there really was no excuse except that he couldn't *not* look at her. The sight of her was better than a sunset to fill up his soul. That's when he realized the fantasy of carrying her off didn't just happen when they were in the same room. He'd been alone all afternoon and thoughts of her wouldn't go away. Worse, he'd missed her.

She was a lethal combination of smart, beautiful, sexy and serene. The need to touch her bordered on painful. But seeing her scarred leg had hit him like a bucket of ice water. Life had kicked her in the teeth and he was her boss. Doing what his body was urging him to do would be wrong for those two reasons alone, and he could think of a dozen more. He would not compromise her.

Finally, she finished and rolled up her yoga mat before heading inside. Cal needed fresh air and a drink, not necessarily in that order. Somehow he managed to pour a Scotch and get outside without spilling it. He had just settled in one of the chairs and taken a sip of his drink when Justine came back outside.

"Cal? Your cell rang and I answered." Looking apologetic, she walked over and held out the device. "It's your mother."

He barely held in a groan and hesitated as if she was giving him a snake that would take a painful bite. No guts, no glory, he thought before taking the device. "Hi, Mom."

"Hello, Cal. How are you?"

"Good." If *good* was defined by lusting after his executive assistant. "How are you? Everything okay?"

"Excellent."

"Is Dad all right?"

"Fine. And so are your brothers and sister and your niece. And now that the pleasantries are out of the way, I have to ask about the young woman who answered your phone."

"That's Justine, my—" He'd almost said *employee* but remembered just in time about the bet. He wasn't supposed to be working. If Katherine Hart found out he was, that sweet classic car would never be his. Worse, the family would never let him live this down.

"Your what, dear?"

"Friend. We met here at the resort." That was true.

"She sounded so professional." There was a note of suspicion in his mother's voice.

"She works as an executive assistant and that requires phone skills, so it's probably just her habit to be that way when she's on the phone."

"Even on vacation?"

"I know, right?" Cal neither confirmed nor denied.

"She has a lovely phone voice," Katherine observed.

Everything about her was lovely, but he wasn't telling his mom that. Especially since Justine's door was open and she could overhear. Cal knew this was Katherine's way of trying to get information out of him. He figured it was a mom thing but that didn't make it any less irritating.

"Justine has many fine qualities," he finally said in an attempt to pacify her.

"How did you two meet?"

It was like this woman could read his mind and knew he was lying, if not outright then in spirit. How was he going to respond without an actual falsehood?

"Believe it or not, Mom, I opened the door to the villa

where I'm staying and there she was. Turns out that someone at registration sent her here."

"It's a sign," said his mother, the romantic, the matchmaker, the woman who believed that love truly did conquer all. It was probable that she also believed unicorns were real. "Maybe you two are meant to be."

Not likely. The attraction was probably him being punished for some horrible crime against karma. "She's a very special woman," he said sincerely.

"I'm so glad you met someone to spend time with on your vacation. What have you been up to?"

"Well, I went skydiving." That was before Justine and seemed like a lifetime ago.

There was a groan from the other end of the line. "I can't believe you jumped out of a perfectly good airplane on purpose."

Hmm. Justine had said something similar. Although she'd called him a sanity-challenged, adrenaline junkie thrill seeker. "Believe it."

"Obviously you lived to tell about it," she said wryly. "But that is not my idea of a good time."

As it turned out, she was right. A broken leg wasn't much fun. But he wasn't going to mention that part. Not only had it resulted in him violating the spirit of the wager with his brother, the information would worry his mother needlessly.

"It was actually exhilarating." Until the hard landing.

"Please tell me that Justine's interests run to safer, less adventurous activities."

Justine had actually called his pursuits life-threatening but that was irrelevant to this conversation. "She has scheduled things to do that don't require one's feet to leave the ground."

"I'm liking her more and more," Katherine said enthusiastically. "Tell me all about it."

This wasn't new for her. Some of his earliest memories involved this woman encouraging him to talk about things. But for some reason, this time bugged him more than it usually did. This was more of an inquisition. He imagined a hostile witness felt this way when an attorney was trying to trip him up and reveal more than intended.

"Are you spying on me for Sam?"

"No." There was a long pause. "Yes. Well, spying, maybe, but Sam didn't put me up to it. I'm concerned and want to know that you're relaxing, recharging your batteries."

He wasn't, but that was his own fault. "I'm fine, Mom."

"If you say so." There was a moment of silence before she said, "So tell me what you've been up to."

"Well…Justine convinced me to sit on the beach with a book."

"No," she said, sounding shocked. "You actually sat still long enough to read?"

Not exactly. He'd actually made her sit still long enough to talk. "It was a beautiful day. Sun, sand, sea."

"That sounds lovely. What else?"

"Justine signed me up for a basket weaving class."

"I did that to your father when we were there." Katherine's laugh was full of delight. "I'm pretty sure he's never forgiven me. His finished product looked like a funky coaster."

"I feel his pain." Cal shook his head ruefully but the revelation made him smile. And the memory of that afternoon washed over him, warm and bittersweet. "Justine tried to put an optimistic spin on it—the beginning of an area rug. A place mat for a very small plate."

"She sounds charming."

And so much more, he thought. She had a way of getting him to do things he didn't want to, then wonder why he ever thought it would be so bad. Or maybe just doing them with her made all the difference in the world. He wasn't willing to find out which.

"She's very pleasant company," he finally said.

"Oh, Cal—" Katherine sounded disappointed in him. "You're still doing it."

"What?"

"Keeping women at a distance."

Just this one, he thought. When he looked at his marriage, he could trace the reason for failure back to his decision to move forward with the woman who'd loved his brother first. He was in that place now with Justine, at a crossroads. The path that brought them together was riddled with land mines and the one that they traveled separately kept everyone safe. That's the one he planned to take, for her sake. And maybe a little for his.

"Let it go, Mom. I'm on vacation."

"You're right. And it sounds like you're having a wonderful time. I'm so glad."

"So you're going to stop worrying about me?"

"Fat chance." She laughed. "I'll just keep it to myself."

"Fat chance," he said back. But he wouldn't have it any other way.

Cal chatted with her a couple more minutes before ending the call. He set the phone on the table and finished his Scotch, thinking about how his assistant had been a big part of the conversation. He wasn't sure what that meant.

And speaking of her, she poked her head out the door and asked, "Is everything okay?"

No, he wanted to say. He'd missed her today and dinner was lonely. None of that came out of his mouth. "You are in so much trouble."

She moved outside and sat in the chair beside his. "I wasn't sure whether or not to answer. The caller ID came up as private and I didn't know who it was. I thought it might be important, so—"

"My mom wanted to know all about the professional-sounding woman who answered my phone."

"Oh, Cal—" She looked upset. "I hope I didn't ruin anything for you."

"The wager is secure." He stretched his bad leg out in front of him. "And I really need to thank you."

"Why?"

"If you hadn't bullied me into leisure activities I would have had to lie outright instead of tweaking the truth. So I'm grateful to you." But much less thankful for how hot she looked in the yoga clothes she still wore.

"I'm glad. So in addition to relaxing you, the excursion gave you cover." She met his gaze. "You missed a good one today. The island is beautiful. The guide took me up to the highest point and you could see everything. It was absolutely spectacular."

And you're an idiot, he filled in silently. That was probably true and wouldn't be the first time. The real question was how he moved forward. He had two options. Send her back to Blackwater Lake and soldier on alone or tough it out for the next two weeks.

Both had a downside. He'd undertaken projects that were time-sensitive, and bringing in another assistant—assuming anyone would accept the job—would be challenging. It would be time-consuming to get them up to speed. And the fewer people who knew he was violating the spirit of the wager, the better.

If he changed nothing, he would have to continue to keep Justine at a distance, and every day his willpower was tested in new and different ways.

But with two weeks left until he won the bet, the smart move was to put on his big boy pants and stay the course. Even if it killed him.

Vacation really sucked.

Two days after the phone call, Justine was done feeling guilty about answering Cal's cell and forcing him to explain her to his mother. Ever since then he'd been crabby and monosyllabic. If he'd been that way when she first arrived to work for him, it would be easier to deal with now, but that wasn't the case. In the beginning he'd treated her to his charm and sense of humor. The boss he'd turned into since seeing her scarred leg was like Mr. Hyde to Dr. Jekyll. She'd nearly used up all of her grit trying to pretend things were normal, but maybe she could manage to dredge up just a little more.

"I think this chicken might just be the best I ever had." She was sitting at the villa's dining table to Cal's right.

"It's like shoe leather."

"Maybe it's just the piece you got," she said, putting as much cheer as possible into her voice. "I'll switch with you."

"No. It will do." Without looking at her he took another bite.

She, on the other hand, had to bite her tongue to keep from calling him a martyr. "I was thinking about ordering dessert tonight. George was telling me about a cobbler the chef does with fruit grown here on the island. In fact, I saw the fields on the tour the other day."

His scowl turned a little darker at the mention of her solo excursion. "No dessert for me. With this damn cast on I can't work out."

"You told me the cast is coming off in a week. How much weight can you really put on?"

"Easy for you to say, being in such good shape." He looked at her then and his gaze dropped lower to the region of her chest. That didn't make him happy because it appeared he gritted his teeth before saying, "Order it for yourself if you'd like."

"I wouldn't eat it in front of you."

"Then I'll leave. Maybe go out on the patio to count my breaths and fill up my soul with sunset. There are no calories in that. No harm, no foul."

That did it. Justine put her fork down. "Cal, what's going on with you?"

"I have no idea what you're talking about."

Even though he looked her in the eye, she knew he was lying, that he was painfully aware of the situation. There was a subtle note in his voice. It had been there when he was on the phone with his mother and playing fast and loose with the truth. Part of her wondered when she'd gotten to know him so well, and the other part wished he was a complete stranger and easy to ignore. But the truth was, she liked him. A lot. Not this petulant, self-centered man as much, but she knew another side to him. One that was generous, kind and understanding. What had happened to send that man into hiding?

"I am many things," she said, "but a stupid fool isn't one of them. You've disappeared into your man cave."

"On the contrary, I'm sitting right here. And I have always been visible."

"The cave thing was a metaphor and you know it. You've been different for the last couple of days."

"I disagree. Maybe you're the one who's different."

That was probably true, but not the way he meant it. She had changed since meeting him. For the first time since losing everything, she was ready—no, eager—to live again. The difference in her attitude was Cal.

"No. I'm right about this," she insisted. "You haven't badgered me into keeping you company on the beach. Or tried to talk me into going to dinner. I have no illusions about another basket weaving class, but you didn't look this peeved when I was sure you were going to fire me. Even that would be better than pacing around mumbling that vacation sucks."

"You heard that?"

"Yes. The richness of life is about the effort you put into living it. If anyone knows that, it's me."

"Next you'll be preaching that when life gives you lemons make lemonade." He tapped his lip. "Or the ever-popular 'It's always darkest before the dawn.'"

"I was trying to avoid clichés." She could tell he was fighting a smile. At least that was a somewhat positive reaction, but why did he feel the need to suppress his amusement? Could be because sharing humor was a form of intimacy and that's what he was resisting. "What are you thinking?"

"That answering your question crosses a boss/employee line."

"Kind of late to draw that distinction now, don't you think?" They'd already shared a lot of personal details about their lives.

He pushed his plate away, the food barely touched. "It's a distinction that should have been drawn in the beginning. My bad."

"So you expect me to forget all that?" Disregard the way he looked at her with a hungry intensity that took her breath away?

"Pretend it never happened."

That was impossible. "That would be like trying to put glitter back in a bottle."

"Try." His voice had an edge and there was an expression in his eyes that hovered somewhere between anger and frustration. And warning.

"This doesn't make sense. Did I do something? You never had a problem before telling me if you were irritated by whatever I did. The second day I was here you were deeply annoyed because I refused to work overtime. Since when did you start holding back?"

He opened his mouth to say something, then shook his head and stood. "I'm going to sit outside on the patio and silently count my breaths. If my soul gets a refill in the process, well, that's okay, too. For sure it will be quiet."

"I think you just told me to mind my own business."

"However you interpret that is your call." Almost as an afterthought he grabbed the crutches, only to keep weight off the injured leg for the prescribed length of time, she guessed. His balance was excellent and he probably didn't need them now, so close to the cast coming off. He went to the French doors, then moved through the opening to sit beside the pool.

Left alone, Justine was angry and hurt. She stood and started pacing. There were so many thoughts and feelings swirling inside her that she couldn't sit still. And there was an *aha* moment while she was at it. When she was in such a dark place after the accident, well-meaning family and friends told her to keep putting one foot in front of the other. Live life to the fullest. She could be happy again and going through the motions would put her back on the road to normal.

All she heard was *blah, blah, blah*. Platitudes she disregarded. How frustrating it must have been for the people who cared about her and were only trying to help. Right now, this moment, she knew how it felt to try to get through to someone who refused to listen. It was damned annoying and she made a mental note to apologize to friends and family for her behavior.

And speaking of advice, she remembered giving the room service waiter relationship advice, telling him to be honest and open about his feelings. If Justine did less than that, she'd be a do-as-I-say, not-as-I-do kind of person. Your basic hypocrite.

She stopped walking and looked out the French doors to the patio bathed in twilight. Perimeter lights showed Cal sitting with his back to her, broad shoulders tensed as he presumably counted his breaths. If she told him exactly what she was thinking he might just fire her for real. The second day of work, when she defied his order, she'd ignored his irritation and was still here, but if she was honest now and he went with the nuclear option, she might very well be packing her bags. Still, saying nothing would drain her soul to the point it might never be filled up again.

Before she could change her mind, she marched outside and stopped beside his chair. "I have something very important to say to you."

"Damn it."

"What?" The knot in her stomach expanded painfully.

"I lost count of my breaths."

Under different circumstances that would have made her laugh. "I have to say what's on my mind or my head just might explode."

"Okay, then, but—"

"No *buts*. There's something going on between us. And don't tell me it's business because I know better. It's personal and—"

"Could it be you're imagining things?" Might be wishful thinking, but that sounded like desperation in his voice. He was trying to dodge the issue.

"Look, Cal, I'll be the first to admit that I'm out of practice with this sort of thing." She thought about that for a moment. "I guess, technically, I was never in practice since I got married pretty young, but…" She took a big breath and pushed on. Couldn't stop now. "I think you're attracted to me."

"And why do you think that?" The words were meant to mock, but there was a ragged edge that stripped away the sarcasm. It almost sounded as if he was running out of places to hide.

"I haven't forgotten how a man looks at a woman when he wants her. And I'm almost positive you've been looking at me that way."

"Justine, it would be best if you stop—"

"No. This has to be said. I've *seen* you look at me that way, until you wouldn't look at me at all. But you're my boss, and a good one in spite of what the clerical staff thinks." She was trying to cut the tension with humor, but judging by his strained expression, it wasn't working. *In for a penny, in for a pound*, she thought. "I know you walk a fine line and might think it's inappropriate to cross it. That would be the case if I didn't want you to cross it, too."

"Justine, please—"

She barreled on before the warning in the way he said her name could take hold. "But then I realized that you changed after I told you about what happened to my family. If you're worried about offending me because of that, don't be. It took a while, but I've realized something and you should know this."

"What's that?" He was looking down, then met her gaze.

"They'll always be in my heart, but they're gone and never coming back. No matter how much I wish I could change it. But I know they would want me to move for-

ward and be happy." She sighed. "If the situation was reversed, that's what I would want."

He hadn't fired her yet. But then, he hadn't exactly
commented, either. Trying to stop her didn't count. Suddenly her legs felt as if they wouldn't hold her up, so she
sat on the chair beside him.

"You told me once that you didn't do things that you're
not good at. Rumor has it that you've had sex with a lot of
women, so one could assume that you're good at it." She
twisted her fingers together nervously, then linked her
hands, settled them in her lap and stared there instead of
at him. "Here's the thing, Cal. I'm pretty sure I've been
looking at you the same way you've been looking at me."

"Justine," he nearly groaned, and that couldn't be a
good thing.

"In case that wasn't clear enough—I want you, Cal.
That's a very big line to cross, but I'd be willing to bet
you've been crabby because you feel the same way but
you're afraid of hurting me somehow. Either because of
my past or the fact that I work for you." She looked at him
then. The jerk of a muscle in his jaw hinted at a conflict
raging inside him. "I really wish you would say something. Preferably not about firing me."

He met her gaze, and the darkness in his was a little
frightening. "Please go back inside, Justine."

"But—"

"Please. Now," he begged.

She heard, *Pack your bags and go.* Something broke
inside her and she couldn't stop the words. "Why don't
you want me?"

Chapter Ten

Justine was horrified and humiliated by what she'd said. She had to get away. Now. "I'm sorry. That was—"

A sob choked off her words and she stood, blindly turning away with tears stinging her eyes. Then she felt Cal's big hand curve around hers before he gently tugged her into his lap.

"Justine—what am I going to do with you?"

She blinked furiously, trying not to cry and make this worse than it already was. "You could start by not pitying me."

"Is that what you think?"

"Among other things." Their faces were inches apart but she couldn't look at him. She wouldn't be able to stand it if she broke down. That would take this horrifying, humiliating scene to a whole new level of awful.

Cal cupped her face in his hands and forced her to meet his gaze before tenderly touching his mouth to hers. His lips were soft and warm, gentle and sweet. It both shocked and charmed her. If this moment never ended that would be all right with her. As soon as that thought flashed through her mind, he stopped kissing her, but instead of pulling away, he rested his forehead against hers.

"I don't pity you. In fact, I'm a little annoyed that you didn't recognize me being noble."

"What I got was you being a gigantic jerk." She stared at him and decided it didn't really matter what she said. After this she was probably getting booted out of here anyway. "You were distant and kind of jackass-y."

Amazingly, he grinned. "Don't hold back. Tell me how you really feel."

His smile seeped inside and warmed her in places that had begun to freeze and shrivel. "I feel as if Cal Hart disappeared right after I showed off the scars on my leg and told you about losing my family. There was no explanation from you. Just radio silence."

"Jackass-y?" he asked.

"Exactly. Obviously you were repulsed by how my leg looks. How is that noble?"

"You've got it all wrong." He slid both arms around her waist and snuggled her a little closer. "I think you're beautiful—inside and out. And I wanted you. When you showed me the scars and told me how you got them, I still wanted you. That was a problem. Because seeing the signs of trauma to your leg made what happened to you real for me. It seemed wrong to make a move, and I didn't want you to feel awkward what with working together or anything else."

"So you disappeared?"

"I was protecting you," he protested.

"From yourself," she clarified.

"Yes. If I hadn't pulled back, there's no way I could resist touching you, and that would make it impossible not to have you." Sincerity and longing darkened his eyes.

"You wanted me?" She couldn't quite believe what she was hearing even though she'd suspected. Now she was almost afraid to believe it was true.

He kissed her and whispered against her lips, "I've wanted you from the moment I first saw you."

"That's hard to believe. I've read about your dalliances. Every last woman was beautiful and perfect."

"No one is perfect," he said.

"The women you dated came pretty close."

He studied her. "Sounds like you're having second thoughts."

"Not really. I'm just giving you an exit plan."

"What if I don't want one?" He took her hand and lifted it to his lips. "In case you're still not convinced, I'll make this as clear as I know how. I want you more than I've wanted any woman. Ever."

"Oh, Cal—" She could hardly breathe. It felt as if he'd just plucked the brightest star from the sky and handed it to her. Shyly, she met his gaze. "There was a time when I didn't believe I'd ever be happy again. Even for a moment. But I am right now."

"Good."

"But—" She hesitated, then figured she might as well get it all out there. "I'll be honest. I haven't done this for a long time. There's been no one since my husband. I'm a little nervous."

"If it makes you feel any better, now I'm nervous."

"I'm not worried. You don't do anything you're not good at." He'd said that about marriage, but she was pretty sure he'd made no such vow about sex. "I hope I'm not a disappointment."

"You never could be. And, just so you know, this is my first time with a cast on my leg. There will be logistics."

The heat of his gaze warmed her skin and started tingles dancing inside her. "I think I can handle logistics."

"That's my girl."

Cal kissed her with a little more intensity. More focus.

As if now that they'd made their intentions and expectations clear, he was making his move. Finally. He kissed her mouth, her nose and cheek, then nuzzled her hair aside and went to work on her neck. She was pretty happy about that when she shuddered in the most delicious way, just before he caught her earlobe between his teeth.

She gasped with pleasure. "Oh, boy—"

"You like that?" he whispered.

"That is a big two thumbs-up."

So he did it again, then blew softly on the moistness he left behind. The sensation drove her crazy and made her shiver. His hand at her waist, he moved his thumb and brushed it back and forth on the underside of her breast. Even through the material of her dress and bra, the touch had excitement blasting to every part of her body.

He was kissing her neck and smiled against her skin. "I feel your pulse racing."

"It definitely is."

She felt him touch her back. Then the zipper on her dress slowly lowered. When it was at her waist, she shrugged her arms out of the bodice and let it pool in her lap. A balmy, light breeze caressed her naked shoulders as Cal cupped her almost bare breast. Rubbing his thumb lightly across the peak made it tighten in response. With a desperation that was heady and new, she wanted to feel his hand on her bare skin. Then a cloud drifted over the nearly full moon, throwing them into shadow for a moment.

It was enough to remind her they were outside, not so far from the sand, where anyone might walk by. "How private is the beach?"

"Very private." He met her gaze, his eyes searching hers. "But you're uncomfortable."

"Yes."

"Can't have that. Stand up," he ordered.

She did, and he reached out to slide her dress down to a puddle of material at her feet, leaving her in just her bra and panties. "I can't believe you just did that. What if someone walks by?"

"First, that was logistics in action. Second, no one will see us. But if they did, you could be wearing a bikini." His eyes grew hot as he stared at her. "I lost track of how many times I thought about you swimming out here and wondering how you looked in a bathing suit."

"In case there's any question, I'm not a *Sports Illustrated* swimsuit model. That's got to be a disappointment—"

"Oh, sweetheart—believe me, I'm the exact opposite of disappointed."

The words and husky, heartfelt tone made her heart soar. She stepped out of the dress and picked it up. "Your room or mine?"

He retrieved his crutches from the ground beside the chair and stood. "Surprise me."

"Logistics will be easier in yours, since you're used to it."

"The condoms are there, too."

Justine felt her cheeks flush with embarrassment. "I forgot about that."

"I didn't." He pointed with a crutch to the French doors opening to his suite in the villa. "Ladies first."

Her heart was beating so fast she could hardly catch her breath. "Okay. I'll turn down the bed."

"And I'll enjoy the view."

There was a sexy male satisfaction in his voice that somehow nudged her confidence further into positive territory. As she moved in front of him, she barely gave a thought to the limp she normally struggled to hide.

He'd seen her flaws—the uneven gait, the disfiguring scars—and wanted her in spite of that. It was a precious gift. Walking in front of him, she smiled.

The room was dark, so she flipped a switch just inside the door and a standing lamp in the corner bathed everything in soft light. Even though her confidence was up, dim lighting was definitely her friend. The layout was a mirror image of her suite—king-size bed, matching nightstands on either side, dresser and armoire. She hurried to fold the thick comforter down along with the blanket and sheet.

Cal moved to her where she stood by the bed. He rested his crutches on the bench at the foot, then sat down on the mattress.

"Come here," he said, his voice deep and edgy.

"Okay."

When she did, he took her hand and pulled her between his legs, then reached behind her back and unhooked her bra. He peeled it off, and before her modesty to cover herself kicked in, he cupped her breasts in his hands. Modesty was highly overrated, she thought, given how good the touch felt.

"Beautiful," he breathed. "And that doesn't do you justice."

She couldn't have responded even if she wanted to, what with the erotic things he was doing to her. He brushed his thumbs over her nipples, then took one into his mouth. Electricity crackled through her and settled low in her belly. She moaned and her breaths came in little gasps. Feeling light-headed, she put her hands on his broad shoulders to steady herself. But the width was a solid reminder of how powerful his body was, so at odds with the gentle way he stroked her.

He lavished attention on her other breast until she was

quivering with need. And then he dropped his hands lower, fingers toying with the waistband of her panties. She held her breath as he hooked his thumbs and drew them down, over her thighs, knees and ankles. He curved his fingers at her hips and urged her closer, then kissed the underside of each breast, her midriff and belly, slowly moving lower.

She didn't think she could take much more and was about to tell him so when he grabbed her playfully and pulled her down onto the bed beside him.

"I've got you now," he said, laughing.

"Right where I want me." She dragged her index finger over the T-shirt covering his chest, then frowned. "You still have all your clothes on."

"So I do."

He took care of that faster than she would have expected, what with the bum leg and all. He also retrieved a condom from the nightstand drawer and put it on. Then he lay back and pulled her on top of him.

"This is logistics," he said and shrugged.

Justine smiled, and it felt extraordinarily tender. He was so adorable she thought her heart might explode. "I'll show you logistics."

She straddled him, then slowly lowered her hips, positioning herself over his thickness. Slowly she took him inside her and sighed with satisfaction at the joining of their bodies. It had been so very long and she hadn't realized how much she'd missed this intimacy. The gratification of being held by a man and making love with him.

She stayed still for several moments, letting their bodies grow accustomed. Then Cal slid his hand up the inside of her leg and brushed his thumb over the bundle of nerve endings at the juncture of her thighs, the most sensitive of places. The touch was like lightning and she gasped at the sizzle of sensation that made her toes curl. He arched into her and lifted her hips up and down, slowly at first, then faster. Before she was ready, pleasure built to the breaking point and exploded through her.

When she collapsed on his chest, he held her as the delightful tremors rocked her world. When she pulled herself together, she started to move again. For him. In moments he went still and groaned, hands reaching for her, pulling her to him while he found his release. The sound of their panting breaths filled the room as they held each other.

Justine had no idea how long they lay there, arms around each other, moonlight spilling inside, the distant sound of waves lapping against the shore. She just knew this couldn't be more perfect.

Playfully she dragged a finger over the dusting of hair on his chest. "I'm glad you didn't fire me tonight."

He rubbed a strand of her hair between his fingers. "Never crossed my mind."

"I thought it might happen."

"Then why did you push the issue?" he asked.

"Because you were acting weird. Walking around like you wanted to put your fist through the wall and mumbling about how much vacation sucked."

He grinned and settled his palms on her thighs, still straddling him. "All things considered, it doesn't suck anymore."

"That's a relief."

"However, I am starving."

She nodded. "Because you were pouting earlier, just before you threw a tantrum and walked out before eating dinner."

"I'm not comfortable with the pouting and tantrum parts of that, but the rest is essentially true." Without warning, he tumbled her to the bed and leaned over to kiss her, and they were a little breathless when he pulled back. "That was for making fun of me."

"Ooh, I'll have to think of more insults."

"I'll help. But first I think we should call room service."

"Excellent idea," she said.

Technically she was working and not on vacation, but her situation definitely didn't suck. It felt balanced. And as close to heaven as one could get on earth. Paradise, indeed.

Cal felt movement in the bed beside him and opened one eye. Sunshine streamed into the room and Justine was curled up next to him. Memories of making love to her flashed through his mind and he smiled. He was pretty sure the look on his face would give sunshine a run for its money in the brightness department.

Not wanting to wake her, he stayed very still and simply looked at her—the full mouth, delicate nose splashed with freckles, strands of beautiful red hair tickling his chest. A feeling of satisfaction and contentment stole over him, a sensation he'd never experienced before. Maybe it was because he'd been so sure he would never have her and something about that felt so wrong. And yet, after carbo-loading on a late dinner last night, he'd had her several more times—each more mind-blowing than the last.

He'd always thought it a romantic cliché that you could never get enough of another person, but that thought crossed his mind now as he stared at her. Silly. This was an interlude, nothing more.

"Are you going to ogle me all morning? Or are you going to order room service?" Her voice was raspy from sleep and incredibly sexy. She opened one eye. "I'm starving."

"For me?"

"Someone's ego got a shot of adrenaline last night." She smiled tenderly and moved closer, touching her lips to his collarbone. After that she gave him a mysterious look. "I'm starving for many things. You might make the list. If you buy me food."

"Breakfast in bed with a beautiful woman. Vacation is getting better and better."

After she gave him the extension for room service, he picked up the phone on the nightstand, then called and ordered. Since they'd shared meals for the last couple of weeks, he knew her favorites and ordered all of them.

He hung up the phone, then reached for her. "Your wish is fulfilled, my lady."

She sat up suddenly, then remembered she was naked and pulled the sheet up to cover her breasts. The gesture was adorable, if unnecessary, since he'd seen and kissed every part of her all night long.

"Cal, there's a problem."

He met her troubled gaze. "Not from where I'm sitting."

"Be serious. I have to let the waiters in. That's what I always do."

"George and William can handle it," he assured her.

"But we don't have clothes on. We can't just let them in here—" She waved a hand to indicate the large bedroom. "They'll know what happened."

"They probably already suspect."

"No, they don't." There was feminine denial in her tone. Also adorable. "Why would they?"

"They're guys. Men know the way another man looks at a woman he wants."

"And you looked at me like that?" Her face took on a pleased expression.

"Yes." He tugged on the sheet, pulling it away. "They noticed."

"But unless they come in here, there's no way for them to confirm. I'm getting dressed to answer the door."

He liked looking at her just the way she was. "Is there any way to talk you out of that?"

She thought for a moment. "I could answer the door without getting dressed."

"That's a big negative." He sighed. "All right. If you must. No one can say I'm not self-sacrificing."

"A prince of a guy." She rolled out of bed, grabbed his shirt off the floor and slipped it on. "I'll be back."

"Promise?"

"Yes." She smiled at him, then was gone.

And the sun seemed not as bright. Wow, that was sappy. But true.

And then other thoughts crept in. Such as—maybe Justine wasn't comfortable having breakfast in bed. It might be too soon for that. As her boss, he'd crossed a line and couldn't go back even if he wanted to. But he wouldn't do anything to make her ill at ease, either. She was putting on clothes, so he would, too. After a quick shower.

About thirty minutes later she wheeled a fully loaded food cart into his suite, where he was dressed and scrolling through messages on his cell phone.

She stood beside the bed with a hand on her hip, looking pretty and casual in a long flowered dress and sandals. "Seriously, omelets? Crepes? Eggs over easy, medium, hard and scrambled? Bacon, sausage *and* ham? Eggs Benedict?"

"You were right here when I called."

"I know—" She sighed. "Apparently I'm a visual person and seeing the volume is—wow."

"And you're responsible for eating half of this," he said seriously.

"You are incorrigible."

"That's what the principal always said when I got sent to the office." He patted the bed beside him. "I just didn't want to miss any of your favorites. And there are so many."

"Someone is feeling his oats this morning." She set out plates on the quilt he'd pulled up. "There should be something on the menu for an occasion like this."

"Breakfast for honeymooners?"

"That's not what we are. I was thinking more a tryst tasting. A sampling of different items instead of the full order to be enjoyed the morning after the night before."

"An excellent marketing idea. We should suggest it to someone."

When the food was all set out, she climbed into the bed beside him. "Without telling that someone how the idea happened."

"Why? It's not an illicit affair. Neither of us is married—" He kicked himself when her smile slipped a little. "I'm sorry. I didn't mean to bring up…anything." He shrugged, not quite sure what to say.

"You didn't. Like I said last night, I've reconciled my past and I'm moving on." She looked at the array of food that filled nearly every square inch of the king-size bed, leaving only enough room for them to sit. "Let's eat before it gets cold."

"Excellent idea."

They each picked up a dish and sampled it, then fed bites to each other. This was their method of working through the array of entrées, fruit and side dishes of potatoes. When neither of them could eat another bite, they leaned back against the pillows and groaned.

"That was too good, but I'm stuffed," Justine said.

"The idea of a sampler is very appealing right about now. Or—" he glanced sideways at her "—someone could have used some self-control with the menu."

"Don't look at me, hotshot. That was all you." She pointed at him. "And it was very sweet of you."

"Glad you think so. Tomorrow morning we'll approach breakfast after the night before a little differently."

A lovely shade of pink colored her cheeks at the suggestion that he would be sleeping with her again later. It wasn't a suggestion, actually, but more of a fact. Resisting her was impossible. He could hardly wait to wake up with her beside him again.

"And by approaching breakfast differently, what you really mean is that I'll be ordering, right?"

He grinned. "It's like you can read my mind."

Her eyes were shining with humor that brought out the gold and green flecks. Beautiful. "You say that as if it's a challenge."

"Them's fightin' words." He started to reach for her.

"No." She shrieked and slid away. "There are plates of food everywhere."

His cell phone sounded and he automatically looked at caller ID, though he was prepared to ignore it and kiss her, letting the chips fall where they might. Except he couldn't.

"It's Sam on Skype," he said, then put his finger to his lips, a sign for her not to make a sound. She nodded her understanding.

He hit the talk button and saw Sam's image. "Hey. What's up?"

"Hi. I'm calling to see if you're surviving vacation."

"Uh-huh." Cal didn't believe that for a second. "You're checking up on me."

"Are you accusing me of not trusting you?"

"Yes."

"Okay. You caught me. I want to see that you're really on the island and living up to the bargain you made."

"I am. And that sweet car is mine."

"You expect me to take your word for it?" Sam asked skeptically.

"Okay. Hold on." Cal slid off the bed and retrieved one crutch, then hopped over to the suite's French doors. He aimed the phone away from him and outside, scanning the patio and pool, then the sand and ocean. "Just another day in paradise."

"Nice. Definitely not Blackwater Lake, Montana," Sam said drily.

"No." He loved the charming, picturesque town and friendly people, but on the island he didn't feel alone— lonely—like he did there. Not since Justine showed up anyway. "It's a great getaway spot."

"I still can't believe you took Mom's suggestion of where to go."

"It saved time not to look and I didn't much care. It's a bet." Speaking of his mother… "Have you talked to Mom?"

"No. I've been busy with work."

"And your new wife and daughter. How are Faith and Phoebe? Everyone healthy and happy?"

"Doing great." Sam smiled. "Best thing that ever happened to me. You should give marriage a try—"

"I already did."

"Again, I meant."

No, Cal thought, he shouldn't give it another try. He wasn't very good at it the first time, so it wasn't something he wanted to do again. "I'm glad things are good with you."

"Speaking of healthy, I saw the crutch. Is there something you want to tell me?"

"Skydiving isn't as easy as it looks. The landing is tricky. I broke my leg. Simple fracture."

"Bummer."

"The cast is coming off in a week."

"Good." Sam hesitated a moment. "Knowing you, there were other activities on your agenda equally life-threatening. That bum leg must have put a wrinkle in your plans."

"I'm managing."

"How? By working?" Sam asked suspiciously.

Cal glanced at Justine, who was quietly removing plates from the bed. He felt his pulse jump, not unlike when he'd stepped out of that plane and plummeted toward the ground. Instead of a yes-or-no answer to his brother's question, he said, "I have sat on the beach with a book and taken a basket weaving class. There are guided tours around the island and cooking classes. Massage. Many activities to keep busy."

"Wow. I'm really impressed that you're fulfilling the bargain."

"I'm an honorable man." Cal saw Justine give him a thumbs-down on that declaration. He shrugged. "And I won't hold it against you for checking up on me. If the situation were reversed, I'd have done the same to you."

"That's the way brothers roll," Sam agreed. "I have to run. It's good talking to you, Cal. Take care of the leg."

"Will do. Thanks for calling. See you soon."

He hit the off button and hopped over to Justine, just clearing the last plates and stacking them on the cart. She looked at him and *tsk*ed.

"What did I do?"

"You are morally bankrupt."

"Me?" He pointed to himself.

"Not only are you violating the spirit of the wager, but you deliberately showed your brother the suite, the patio and the ocean, everything except me. That's a lie of omission."

"I can live with that." He curved his hands on her hips and tugged her close, then started sliding the material up with every intention of pulling the dress over her head and dropping it on the floor. "You know, it's not so bad that you got dressed to let in room service."

"Why is that?"

"Because I get to take your clothes off all over again." He kissed her and she kissed him back.

He just couldn't wait until tonight to have her.

Chapter Eleven

Justine was sitting at her desk, trying to be an efficient assistant and failing miserably. It was logical to assume that her concentration at work would improve after sleeping with Cal, because of the whole tension-relieving aspect of it. That seemed to work for him but was definitely not the case for her.

She kept looking at him and marveled that he seemed to have no problem focusing on the work. He wasn't stealing looks at her, and she would know since she couldn't seem to lose the habit of glancing at him all the time. Apparently the ability to concentrate had become his post-sex superpower.

It had been a week. Seven days since she'd bared her soul to him and her body, too. Every one of those nights had been spent in his bed. Maid service was no doubt happy there was only one suite to clean. And Justine was more than content to be in his arms, especially because Cal seemed eager to have her there. On paper she didn't have a care in the world, but deep inside she had a great many cares.

"Do you have the cost projections for the wind farm

project in Maine?" Cal was sitting on the couch as usual and looked up from his laptop when he asked the question.

"They're here on my desk somewhere." Her work space was uncharacteristically cluttered and might just reflect her inner turmoil. She started to go through a stack of papers. "I'll find it."

"No rush. When you can." He looked down at his computer screen again. Displaying his superpower in all its glory.

And Justine studied her own monitor—for the fourth time. The environmental impact study just wasn't especially compelling today for some reason.

"I'm going to take a break," she told him. "Is that all right with you?"

"Of course." He glanced up and smiled, then turned back to work.

It felt like a lifetime ago that he'd pushed back on her taking regular breaks. At the time, making her point seemed a very big undertaking, but it now paled in comparison to what was going on with her boss.

She picked up her cell phone and went into her old suite to stretch and try to clear her mind. That always seemed to help restore her balance and serenity. Both had been sorely tested in the three weeks she'd spent with Calhoun Hart. She'd tried meditation-heavy yoga but her mind kept straying back to him, vacillating between elation and unease.

She decided to do hatha yoga, combining deep breathing with poses to promote flexibility, balance and relaxation. All of those qualities were lacking in her right now.

She was positioning herself when the phone rang. After checking caller ID, she smiled and hit the talk button. It was her good friend and Cal's vacationing assistant. "Hi, Shanna."

"Justine, is this a bad time?"

"No. I'm taking a break."

"I hoped you would be. How are you?"

"Good." The answer was polite but not enthusiastic. When you went to bed with the boss, life tended to get complicated. "How was your cruise?"

"Oh, my God—" There was a pause where her friend was no doubt putting a hand to her chest and wearing a rapturous expression on her face. "It was fantastic. Better. The most awesome trip ever."

"You met someone, didn't you?" Justine guessed.

"How did you know? You're psychic. I always suspected but that's proof."

"I didn't read your mind, but I know you pretty well. That's your I-met-a-man voice."

"I didn't realize I had one. And it's a little scary that you can read me so accurately," Shanna said.

"So, I'm right." It wasn't a question.

"Yes. I did meet the most wonderful man on the entire planet."

Justine could argue that point given the turn in her status with Cal but decided not to go there. "Wonderful, huh? Do you expect me to believe you didn't fall for a cad?"

"Since my pattern is hooking up with bozos, I can see why you'd be skeptical. God knows I've kissed a lot of frogs…but this man is really something special."

Justine sat on the bed. She was hearing something new in her friend's voice. "I know it was a relatively long cruise, but it was short enough to hide flaws if one wanted to."

"I know what you're saying, Justine, and I can't really explain why I'm so sure." She took a deep breath. "His name is Mark Shelton and he's a big-time movie producer from California. He brought his whole family on the trip and it's a big, close family—parents, brothers, sisters, their spouses and children."

"Wow. Very generous."

"I know, right?" There was an ecstatic squeal from the other end of the line. "You can really get a sense of a man seeing him with the people who know him best. He's a good guy and they love him. He's great with the kids. I watched him in the pool with them and the nieces and nephews just adore him. He even took care of his sister's infant. That was a seriously take-no-prisoners moment when I saw him holding a baby. Be still my heart."

"Shannie, I have to ask. How can you be sure it wasn't an act for your benefit? He's Hollywood, after all."

"I get it," Shanna said. "I was skeptical, too, and watching carefully, waiting to catch him. But you can't fake the baby thing and the kids weren't coached. We both know children do not suffer fools or filter comments when something pops into their mind. His nieces and nephews just blurted things out like, 'Remember when you took us to the snow?' or, 'I loved when you dug a hole in the sand and buried me.'"

"So you're convinced he's the real deal?"

"Not a doubt. His parents and siblings are genuine, too. He's very close to them."

"Is he the one, Shan?"

"Yes."

"And you're his Ms. Right?"

"Yes. When you know, you just know." Shanna sighed happily. "You know?"

"Yes."

It seemed like another lifetime, but Justine remembered falling in love, that uncomplicated feeling of pure joy at finding the one man she wanted to be with forever. She'd been so young and it was all so easy because she never thought that anything bad could touch them. Until it did.

"I've never been so happy," Shanna gushed.

Justine had been that happy once. When it was so cruelly and suddenly snatched away she'd believed loneliness was all she would have for the rest of her life. She'd never expected someone like Cal.

"But he lives in California, right?"

"Yes."

"And you…don't," Justine pointed out rationally. "I hate being the voice of reason, but just how are you going to work this out?"

"You sure know how to let the air out of the excitement balloon and throw water on the fire of romance, don't you?"

"What are friends for?" she teased. "But seriously, you and Mark must have talked about the geographic consequences of a long-distance relationship."

"More than talked," Shanna confirmed. "We made a decision that it wouldn't work. He proposed and I accepted. I'm moving to California."

"Wow." Even though Justine had suspected that this was where her friend was headed, she was still shocked. "Congratulations."

"Thanks."

"That means you'll have to give Cal your notice."

"I know, and I'm not looking forward to that." For the first time her friend's enthusiasm slipped. "He's driven, but still a great guy and a good boss. I'll miss him."

"But you just moved to Blackwater Lake," Justine protested.

"Yes, I did. On the bright side, half of my stuff is still packed and in storage. And my moving mojo is still going strong." There was another silence on the other end of the line and her friend was probably chewing nervously on her lip. "Be happy for me, J."

"Of course I am," she said quickly. She was also envious. First love was simple, easy and wonderful. "I'm sure you'll be very happy, and I hope I get to meet the man responsible for it."

"You will. Count on it." Shanna blew out a long breath. "I just wanted a break from work. It never occurred to me that I'd find my destiny on vacation."

"Isn't that always the way?" Justine said.

"Speaking of getting away…listen to me going on about myself. How are you?"

"I'm fine."

There was a pause, as if Shanna was waiting for more. "Is that it?"

"What else should there be?"

"For one thing, how is it working with Cal? Worth the big bucks you're getting to put up with him?"

"Since it took you four years to get a vacation, you know better than anyone what he's like."

"That's exactly why I'm asking. Is he driving you crazy?"

Yes, but not the way her friend meant. Their time in bed was sweet, sexy, hot, satisfying. All the more vivid because she'd missed being physically close with a man. But at work, he seemed able to compartmentalize, which should have been reassuring. And it was, in a way. So why wasn't she completely reassured? Probably she needed therapy.

"Justine?"

"Hmm?"

"What's really going on with you and Cal? Is he working you too hard? I warned you not to take this assignment—"

"No. We settled that early on when I threatened to quit. So there's no overtime and I get regular breaks to stretch out my leg." She remembered the intensity in Cal's eyes the first time she'd demonstrated her poses. The thought made her shiver now as it had then and she knew he'd wanted her as badly as she wanted him. And the explosion of desire between them was way better than okay.

"I'm glad you didn't let him walk all over you. But—" An uneasy silence followed that word. "I'm not psychic, either, but I know you and I can hear in your voice that everything's not right. What's going on? A vacation romance for you, too?"

"Why would you say that?"

There was a long silence on the other end of the line. Then Shanna said, "You know the way you know me so well? It works both ways. I nailed it, didn't I? There's something going on between you and Cal, isn't there?"

"Not as dramatic as what's going on with you," she answered.

"No way." Shanna's voice wasn't quite a shriek, but close. "You and Cal? Doing the wild thing?"

Such a fitting way to put it. "Yes, we are mixing business with pleasure," Justine admitted, without detailing the numerous ways he pleasured her every night.

"So, the workaholic has a heart, after all." There was an approving smile in Shanna's voice.

"As you said, he's a good guy when you get to know him. But it's a little soon to talk about heart involvement."

"Hey, I'm engaged to be married and it's been a similar time frame. Is there something I should know?"

"You're asking about love—"

"Duh."

"The answer is that there is no answer. It's still new—"

"What do you want, Justine?"

"That's a good question. We haven't discussed anything, and even if we did—"

"This is me, J. I know you're afraid." Her friend's voice was as gentle and supportive as a hug.

"I prefer to think of it as being unprepared. Even though I made a conscious choice to move on with my life as Wes and Betsy would want, I was thinking in terms of letting myself not be sad anymore. This, with Cal, isn't something I ever expected to face again after losing the people I loved most in the world."

This ambivalence seemed so stupid since she was the one who had opened the door by asking Cal why he didn't want her. Talk about mixed signals.

"You were prepared to be alone but not to face falling in love and the potential pain of it. And I'm not just talking about losing someone the way you did your husband. There are other ways to be hurt. And Cal has baggage."

"I know. He told me about his marriage." The newly reawakened part of her had accepted that living life meant opening herself up to a relationship—the highs, lows and complete mess of it. But now… "You nailed it, Shannie. I think this uneasiness is resistance to potential pain."

"Oh, honey—" Her friend sighed loudly. "I wish I could tell you it will be all right, but there's no way to be sure. So the best strategy I can come up with is this. Just enjoy yourself and don't create problems where there aren't any. Have no expectations and live in the moment."

That made sense. She was making this complicated when it didn't need to be. *Have fun and don't expect more.*

"Excellent advice, Shannie."

Justine truly meant that and planned to take it. She felt as if the weight of the world had lifted from her shoulders.

* * *

"Well, well, well." Cal ended the call with his soon-to-be ex-assistant and looked at Justine working beside him on the sofa. "Shanna said you already know about her engagement and resignation."

"Yes. She called during my break."

It hadn't escaped his notice that she'd come back from that break much lighter of spirit than when she left. He knew that was his fault. Things had changed between them and she would want definition of what was happening. He knew only one way to define it. Simple and straightforward. Being with her was…good.

"She sounded very happy," he said.

"I thought so, too." Justine took off her glasses and tossed them on the coffee table, on the spreadsheet they'd been studying before Shanna called him. "Believe me, I grilled her like raw hamburger. It's a big step to pick up your life and move it to another state. I wanted to make sure she'd given this decision a lot of thought."

"And?"

"She said when you know, you just know."

"Hmm."

Cal knew a lot of things. He liked Justine very much. In fact, he'd go so far as to say he'd never felt this way about a woman, ever. But these circumstances were different. It wasn't the real world, where things had a way of not working out. "For Shanna's sake, I hope what she thinks she knows goes the way she wants it to."

"I agree. On the other hand, I've become a believer in not wasting time."

Because no one knew how much time they had, he thought. That must have been a hard lesson for her. He wanted to scoop her up, pull her against him and make the shadows in her eyes disappear. But this was work time. When he'd crossed the line from professional into personal, he'd promised himself to keep the two separate. It wasn't easy with her looking like temptation in a sleeveless cotton dress. If he was being honest, it wouldn't matter what she wore because he knew every inch of what was underneath. And he couldn't seem to get enough of that.

And that's why he didn't look at her during work hours unless it was absolutely necessary.

"So," Justine said, "you're going to need a replacement for Shanna. Do you want me to start looking through your existing employees? If you don't find anyone, we can open up a wider search."

"That sounds like a good plan." He noticed her giving him a strange look. "What?"

"For a man who barely gave his assistant a day off, you're taking this resignation of your right-hand person remarkably well."

"On the outside," he clarified. "On the inside I'm having a spectacular meltdown."

"No one would ever guess. Maybe your vacation has given you the reserves to keep your inner pouter just where he belongs."

She might have a point about the battery recharge. And in a few days the revitalizing would be over. When he'd arrived, his attitude was resentment, as if he'd been given a time-out even though he'd accepted the bet. He was all about hunkering down and gritting his teeth to get through, to do whatever he had to in order to win. Then he went skydiving. What was that saying? Men plan and God laughs.

He looked his fill at Justine's fresh, pretty, peaceful face and felt his chest grow tight with tenderness. Hurting his leg might just have been the luckiest break he ever got.

"Okay, then," she said. "I'll contact Human Resources in Blackwater Lake and get them going on finding a replacement for Shanna. Then we can finish going over the cost analysis for this project—"

He held up a hand to stop her. "That can wait."

"What?" She blinked at him, obviously surprised.

"Finding another Shanna will work itself out, but we only have a few days left on the island. I think we should take advantage of that and do something fun today."

A slow smile curved up the corners of her mouth before she wiped an imaginary tear from the corner of her eye with a knuckle. "My little boy is all grown up."

"Very funny." He was pretty sure last night in bed he'd shown her exactly how grown up he was, but that's not what she meant. He grinned. "What do you say we go basket weaving again?"

"I say the surprises keep on coming." She was staring at him as if he'd just sprouted another head.

"Let's just say I'm determined to master the skill."

"Your aggressive streak is showing." She thought for a moment. "Competitive basket weaving. Could be an Olympic event."

"You mock me, but never say never. Are you game for it today?"

"Twist my arm." She stood and walked over to the desk to get her purse. "Ready when you are."

After securing transportation, he took her to lunch at the nearby resort. Then they joined a few other guests for the class being held at the picnic table area with a spectacular view of the ocean. The breeze was more than pleasant and the sky an indescribably stunning shade of blue without a cloud in sight. Justine sat beside him, her shoulder brushing his as they laughed and teased. The afternoon was perfect—in spite of basket weaving.

Cal followed directions and carefully wove the reeds together, doing his damnedest to create a functional thing. But his hands felt too big and clumsy. The materials were too unwieldy and delicate.

He stared ruefully at the finished product. "Guess what it is."

"A colander?" Although she tried to look serious, there was laughter in her eyes as she studied the dysfunctional crisscrossing of palm fronds. "There are so many spaces for water to drain."

Frowning, he held up what he'd made—whether for inspection or more ridicule wasn't clear. "There was a time when this being less than perfect would have bothered me. But not anymore."

"Really?"

"Truly. Now I see it as a way to spend an afternoon outside and enjoy the view. Today wasn't about fortunes being made and lost or life and death. Just a pleasant diversion."

"What you're trying to say is that you're relaxed."

"I really am," he agreed.

"So the family intervention was a good thing and made you a vacation convert."

"Yes." He sighed, then looked away from the view and met her gaze. "There's only one downside as far as I can see."

"Oh?"

"I don't want to go back."

Part of that was about wanting to stay in this perfect paradise. But mostly it was about Justine. Leaving would change—this—whatever it was. He couldn't label the feelings and didn't really want to. He just wanted it to *be*. Leaving could and would make everything different, and for reasons he didn't want to examine closely, he wasn't looking forward to that.

"I would say that your time off was a rousing success." She beamed at him as if he was her prize pupil. "Maybe more important—you have learned that work and play are better with balance."

"That's very Zen of you." He studied her. "And you're responsible for making me aware that this is beneficial. You may have noticed that I wasn't very open-minded about this in the beginning."

"No. Really?" She laughed.

"Smart aleck." But he was serious. "I realized that the rest of the world can go on without me for a little while."

"You embraced the message. And it can be life-altering," she agreed.

"There you go being glass-half-full again. You're very good at this whole yoga thing."

"Thanks. Coming from you that's high praise." She looked at the tidy little basket she'd made, then at him. "And it reassures me that my decision to open my own yoga studio was the right one."

"What?" Had she mentioned this before?

"Yes. The whole reason I accepted this assignment with you was the generous salary. That will make it possible for me to open my own business sooner than I'd planned."

"You're abandoning Hart Energy? We just talked about picking up one's life and moving."

"That was about Shanna and getting married. My situation is very different."

"How?"

"For one thing, I've already moved."

And unlike Shanna, she wasn't getting married, he

thought. The *M*-word always put a knot in his stomach. "When did you decide this was what you wanted?"

"I've been planning for this quite a while. It was more than exercise, but a course of therapy that literally got me back on my feet after the accident. I want to pay it forward and help others."

"It's really important to you." That wasn't a question.

She tucked a strand of red hair behind her ear and nodded. "When the announcement was made about the move to Blackwater Lake I started researching the area. There's development happening that will bring in a clientele who will benefit from the lifestyle, service and philosophy I want to provide. Another plus is that there's nothing like it in town. In Dallas there was a yoga studio practically on every corner. And—"

"What?" he asked softly. Her eyes had turned more green than brown, and he had a feeling he knew what she was going to say.

"I needed a scenery change. There were memories everywhere and it seemed like a good idea to move forward in a new place."

"Sounds like you've really thought it through."

"They say you never work a day in your life if you do something you love. For me there's no downside."

For him it felt just the opposite, although Cal couldn't say exactly why that was. He'd been surprisingly okay with Shanna jumping ship, but not so much with Justine doing the same thing. It had nothing to do with work because she hadn't been his assistant in the Blackwater Lake office. Briefly he'd considered offering her Shanna's position but immediately discarded the idea.

Justine was a distraction he couldn't afford on a permanent professional basis. No, his unease was strictly about change. It was the only thing one could count on, but that didn't mean he was okay with it. His instinct was to fix whatever made him uneasy, and he knew from past experience that actions taken under pressure never went well.

Note to self: there is nothing here to fix.

Another note to self: repeat until the first note sinks in.

Chapter Twelve

"I can't believe it. No more plaster leg, no more hobbling around supported by sticks."

It was late afternoon. Justine and Cal had just returned to the villa from the doctor, where he'd had his cast removed. He was ecstatic and grinned from ear to ear.

Justine smiled back. If anyone knew how good it felt to have free use of a limb again, it was her. "At the end you were better than a hobble. Just saying."

Cal spontaneously pulled her into his arms and held her so tight she could hardly breathe. Against her hair he said, "I honestly don't think I could have gotten through this without you, Justine."

"I'm glad I was here."

For so many reasons, but one was completely selfish. Because of him she'd taken a giant step forward in her emotional recovery. She knew now that it was possible for her to be happy again, truly happy and content and not simply pretending for everyone else.

Taking a step back out of his arms, she looked up and met his gaze. "So, it's your last day here. Do you want to tie up loose work ends? Just pack everything up? Or—"

"Are you kidding?" He looked at her as if she'd suddenly turned green. "It's our last day on the island."

"I know. That's what I just said. Where do you want me to focus my time and energy? Organizing paperwork? Making phone calls—"

He touched a finger to her lips to stop the flow of words. "It's our last day on the island. I'm quite sure it's in the vacation convert handbook that on the final day before returning to one's humdrum, mundane life, the inexperienced vacationer must pack as much fun as possible into the remaining hours. Work?" He crossed his fingers, making an X. "Until we're on the plane home tomorrow, whoever says the word *w-o-r-k* will have to pay a forfeit."

"Which is?"

He thought for a moment, then grinned. "A kiss."

"Now there's a deterrent," she scoffed, before standing on tiptoe and touching her mouth to his.

"What was that for?"

"I just banked a forfeit," she said.

"Yeah." He scratched his head. "I'll have to think of something really bad. Like cuddling in the corner."

"Right. A time-out with benefits?"

He shrugged. "We could stand here and debate or go have an adventure."

"Well, you're the one dealing with physical limitations for the last month, so what would you like to do? And before you answer, defining *adventure* would be good. Your last one ended with that leg in a cast."

"Right. No parasailing, hang gliding or rock climbing."

"I knew you weren't just another pretty face. So, what'll it be?"

"I want to walk on the sand, down by the water. Get my feet wet." His blue eyes darkened with focus and it was all directed at her. "With you."

Her pulse jumped once as if to say, *Oh, boy*.

"That sounds like just what the doctor ordered," she said.

"Good. Go put on a swimsuit."

"Why?" she asked suspiciously.

"Because water is wet." It was half statement, half question and all mischief.

"But—" She glanced down at her right leg and realized that covering the scars was always uppermost in her mind.

Cal's expression gentled. "Every single part of you is beautiful. The marks made you who you are, and that's a person I admire and like very much."

"Thank you—"

"I hear a *but* in your voice because you were going to say my good opinion means zilch when a stranger stares at your leg."

Amused now, she folded her arms over her chest. "Was I?"

"Yes. And you know what my response would be?"

"Don't keep me in suspense," she said drily.

"It's late in the afternoon so the beach will be less crowded. And probably someone will see your leg and wonder about it. But you'll never see them again."

She'd expected something along the lines of *You're beautiful inside and out. Let it go. Don't think about that because it doesn't define you.* She'd thought for a moment about pushing back that she might return here for another vacation. Then it hit her that he hadn't meant the statement literally. No one cared about the marks on her body except her. If she didn't give it a thought, neither would anyone else.

"You're absolutely right. Thank you." She stood on tiptoe again and kissed him.

"Are you banking another forfeit?" There was laughter in his eyes.

"No. *Work. Work*," she said. "Now we're back to square one."

They changed into their suits and his look said he clearly approved of her bikini. Then came slathering sunscreen on each other. The touching ignited fires for activities that would keep them indoors, but a sincere need to be in the open air put that on hold.

Justine preferred wearing a sarong, with or without the scars on her leg, unless she was in the water. After putting on her sunglasses, it was time to head out.

Both of them were limping. Cal's injured calf was skinny from lack of exercise and the muscles in Justine's compromised leg protested the exertion of moving through the coarse white sand. They took it slow, and near the water things got easier.

A small wave lapped at their feet and Cal sighed in ecstasy. "I have taken for granted the sheer pleasure of this all my life. Not having something really makes you appreciate what you've been missing."

"And here I thought you were shallow. That was an extremely profound statement, Mr. Hart."

"I have levels," he said proudly.

Justine's comment was deliberately teasing because it was either that or get serious. And she sensed that was the last thing he wanted. Especially during their final hours here in paradise. But he was right about appreciating something you didn't have. She'd missed this closeness with a man, and finding it again truly did make her cherish it. For so long she'd felt that dating was a betrayal of the love she'd had for her husband. Now she knew it validated the relationship she'd lost. That had made her who she was, a woman who was her best self when she gave and received love.

After today she had no idea where this thing with Cal would go. They wouldn't be living under the same roof or possibly even see each other at all. Nothing future had been defined. The unknown was a big, black void, a perversion of this bright, spectacular day with the sun turning the blue water into a carpet of diamonds. So, she was going to do her best not to think about tomorrow.

Strolling slowly, Cal took her hand, a small gesture that seemed as natural as breathing. "I was just thinking—"

"Uh-oh. I thought I smelled smoke," she teased. "I'm not sure I want to hear this."

"Oh, you'll be all over it, Miss Violating the Spirit of the Wager." He smiled down at her.

"I like the sound of that. Continue, please."

"If my brother and my mother hadn't pushed me into this bet, it's quite possible I would never have slowed down long enough to experience a day like this. And I would really have missed that."

"Stop the presses. There's breaking news. Calhoun Hart is waxing poetic and feeling guilty," she added.

"I don't know if I'd go that far. It's just that I feel as if I've gotten so much already. I don't need Sam to pay off the bet." He looked down at her then, but his eyes were hidden by the aviator sunglasses. "This is enough."

Justine's heart pounded and anticipation knotted inside as she hoped he would expand that thought. "Oh?"

But the moment was shattered when a man and woman jogged past and splashed them.

"Oh, God, that felt so good," he said.

Without warning he picked her up and walked deliberately into the ocean. Justine didn't know whether to shriek because she knew what was coming or simply hang on, enjoy the ride and savor this moment being close to him. Before she could make up her mind, he tossed her into the water, then dived in after her.

It was the temperature of bathwater, but salty, clear and beautiful. Cal surfaced, his wide shoulders and broad chest gleaming and gorgeous, wet and wild. What was it about a wet man that made a woman's mouth go dry? But she knew in her heart not just any man would do that to her. Only this one.

She pushed dripping hair off her face. "My sarong is all wet. You're going to pay for that."

"I'm sure it will involve *work*." He moved in close and put his arms around her.

"Forfeit," she cried.

"You got me."

The sun moved lower in the sky and turned the underside of the clouds pink, purple and gold. People walked by but everything disappeared and a perfect moment became the simplicity of their lips touching. It was only the two of them and a balmy breeze caressing their bodies. She could feel Cal's arms tightening around her and his breath coming faster.

Reluctantly he pulled back and drew in a deep breath before releasing it. "Walk on the sand—check. Dip in the ocean—check. Kiss a beautiful woman in the water—check. But I think we should head back to the villa." There was a husky rasp in his voice that said so much more.

"I'll race you," she said. "Last one there is a rotten egg."

He laughed. "Good thing no one is timing us."

They moved from the water to the shore and slowly

walked back, hand in hand. Not many people were out, but an older couple strolled by with their arms around each other's waists. Hellos were exchanged and the silver-haired man and woman smiled indulgently, the way people did at lovers. Justine smiled back, the way people did who envied a man and woman who had grown old together.

That's what she wanted.

The villa came into view and they headed to it, trudging through the sand. Passing the lounges where she'd first convinced him to relax, she thought about how far they'd come since that day she'd helped him to sit.

They moved by the low outside wall, onto the decking where the crystal clear pool was.

Cal stopped and looked down at her. "Lose the sarong. We're going in. After watching you in there night after night, I want to swim with you."

It wasn't easy to untie the wet knot at her waist with shaking hands, but she managed. Then she dived into the water and glided as far as she could go without kicking. Cal did the same and they ended up in the shallow end, just where her feet could touch bottom.

His arms came around her and he smiled in the waning light. "I like swimming with you."

"Technically this isn't swimming, but I can show you some exercises to help rehabilitate the muscle tone in your calf."

"I bet you could." His voice was deep, ragged, seductive.

"However, fair warning," she said, smiling coyly. "It's a lot of *work*."

"I really like forfeit." His smile widened just before his mouth claimed hers.

Wet man, wet kiss. All wow. She was so caught up in

the sensations he was evoking that she hardly felt his fingers unhook her bikini top and strip it away.

"Oh, Cal—"

"Hold that thought."

He pulled himself out of the pool and disappeared inside, then was back faster than one would think a man who'd recently had his cast removed could go. He had a condom and was ready when he walked back into the water and kissed her again. This time her bikini bottom came off and he lifted her. She wrapped her legs around his waist as he entered her.

She was so ready. The walk, dip in the ocean, touching—it all turned her desire into a need so deep it couldn't be denied. Feeling him inside her was all she wanted.

He rocked her against him and kissed her neck, that magical spot beneath her ear. Pleasure exploded inside her and she trembled with the force of it.

Suddenly Cal went still and groaned, holding her tight against him as his release came. They stayed that way for a long time, wrapped in each other's arms.

He cleared his throat. "One more on the list. Making love to you in the pool—check."

She was happy and satisfied, more than she'd been in longer than she could remember. So it was a shock when her eyes filled with tears. Bad things happened in life and you never saw them coming, but tomorrow's departure from here wasn't a surprise. They were going home. That meant things would be different and it made her sad.

The month was over and she wished with all her heart that it didn't have to end.

Late in the afternoon the next day, Cal watched Justine look through every nook and cranny of the villa to make sure she hadn't overlooked anything while packing. He hadn't missed the tears she'd tried to hide after making love in the pool last night. Even though her face was already wet, he'd seen that something was bothering her. He was pretty sure it wasn't something he did, but a guy could never be certain. All he knew was that he didn't like it when she was unhappy.

There was a knock on the villa door and Justine answered it. George and William, their room service waiters, had come to tell her goodbye.

"Thank you so much for everything," she said, hugging each man. "I think I've forgotten how to cook. Maybe you'd like to reconsider my offer to come back to Blackwater Lake with me?"

The taller man laughed. "It is a very tempting offer. But…"

"Yes." She glanced at Cal, then said, "There's always a *but*. Just remember to be honest with the ones you love and communicate."

Cal walked over to shake hands, then gave each of them a generous stack of bills that made their eyes pop. "Your service was exemplary and you will be sorely missed. Thank you for making our stay one that we will never forget."

The shorter man nodded and spoke for both of them. "It has been our pleasure to be of service to you. Please come back and visit with us again soon."

"I would like that very much." Cal watched Justine hug each of them one last time and knew his stay here on the island had been remarkable because of her. She was the light to his darkness. And yesterday she'd cried. Why?

He had a long plane ride home to find out the answer to that question.

When goodbyes were over and the two resort staffers left, he met her gaze. "Are you all set?"

"Yes." But her eyes said just the opposite, even though everything was in her suitcase.

With his hand at the small of her back, they walked out the front door together. The crutches he'd gladly abandoned yesterday rested against the entryway wall, and he'd instructed the front desk to return them to the medical facility. He never wanted to see those sticks again, in spite of the fact that he'd met Justine because of his accident. The silver lining, he thought. She would be proud of him for that positive mental energy.

The town car driver stood by the open rear passenger door. Cal handed Justine inside first, then followed her. The air-conditioning was blasting and took the humidity out of the air, which would make the short drive to the small island airport more comfortable.

But nothing about the drive was relaxed because his companion was unusually quiet and subdued. Patience wasn't his strong suit, but he reminded himself that in a little while they'd have a chance to talk this through.

They exited the car, and Justine looked for a long time at the three-hundred-sixty-degree ocean view. Her eyes were hidden behind large sunglasses, but judging by body language, she wasn't happily anticipating getting on the plane and leaving this place. Cal shared her reluctance, especially since finding out she was planning to resign from Hart Energy.

Before she'd revealed her business plan, he'd been okay with ending their vacation because he would see her at work. Now that wasn't going to be a possibility for very long, forcing a change in his strategy. But every motivational speech he'd ever heard declared that change was just opportunity.

"So, are you ready to be amazed?" he asked. Did he sound as ridiculously cheerful as he thought?

She turned to him. "What?"

"We're getting on the private jet. Prepare yourself once again for luxury overload." That's what she'd said the first day she'd walked into the villa—the plane, the resort. She'd been awed. Her expression didn't reflect that now. "Hey, I'm trying to lighten the mood. Work with me."

She glanced at the Gulfstream waiting nearby, engines at a low hum, then looked back at him and forced a smile. "Very exciting. An adventure."

"That's the spirit."

"Let's roll." She headed for the portable stairway that had been pushed against the aircraft's doorway. Then she stopped and looked at him. "What about the bags?"

"You really don't have much experience with this luxury thing," he scolded gently.

"I promise not to hold it against you that you do." Her sass was a good sign.

"The driver and plane personnel will put our things on board."

"So we don't need to watch and make sure?"

"You can if you want. But this isn't like flying commercial. I'm pretty certain these guys can handle it. Or we'll know who to hold responsible if our luggage is lost." He held out his hand. "After you."

She nodded and walked ahead of him, climbing the stairs before stepping through the doorway into the plush interior. There was a configuration of soft, leather-covered benches, tables and captain's chairs. The galley was in the back and a bar was set up on the port side. A company flight attendant was there to greet them.

"Hello, Brad," Justine said and gave him a friendly smile.

"Good to see you again, Justine." He held out his hand. "Hi, Cal. Hope it was a good month."

The best, he thought. "I have no complaints."

"The flight crew are doing precheck. The captain wanted me to let you know the weather between here and Blackwater Lake looks good. It should be a smooth ride."

"Excellent news." Cal glanced at his companion and thought time would tell whether or not it would be smooth in every way.

"We expect to have clearance soon to take off, so if you'll buckle up…" Brad indicated the two seats just behind him.

"Okay." Cal looked at her. "Window or aisle?"

"I don't care. You pick. It's your plane."

"It's the company plane and I'd really like you to sit where you want."

She took off her glasses and met his gaze. "Window."

"Done." He moved so she could get by him and sit.

She settled in and sighed. "*Comfortable* doesn't even begin to describe this. It's like being cushioned in bubble wrap."

"Not quite the visual they were going for, probably, but true," he agreed.

Shortly after they buckled in, the captain announced he'd received clearance from air traffic control to take off, and they were ready to go. One advantage of a small airport was no line of planes, so it wasn't long before they'd taken off and reached their normal cruising altitude. The seat belt sign went off and they were free to move about the cabin.

"I think we should have a drink." Cal knew that Brad would be serving dinner soon and Justine was clearly tense. Not good when it was the polar opposite of what she'd preached for the last month. And he expected her to say she was *fine*—the four-letter word men universally hated—depending on a woman's tone and expression when she said it.

"A glass of wine would be lovely," she said.

He'd been thinking a tumbler two fingers full of Scotch, but wine would work. He asked Brad to open a bottle of his favorite red. The other man did as requested, then disappeared after pouring the pinot noir into their crystal glasses.

Cal held his up. "What should we drink to?"

She sighed. "I can't think of a thing."

He remembered last night and the sadness on her face when she valiantly tried to hide her feelings. Screw the toast. He couldn't stand one more second of not knowing what was on her mind. "Why were you crying last night?"

Her gaze snapped to his, clearly understanding what he was referring to and surprised that he'd noticed. "Would you believe happy tears?"

"Maybe if you hadn't looked as if there was a permanent ban on ice cream. This may come as a shock, but you're not very good at hiding your feelings." And he was grateful for that. In his experience, that's what women did.

"Wow, I thought being in the pool and all…" She tried to smile. "You are quite observant."

"I try. So, talk to me about why you're not anxious to get home."

She sighed, then met his gaze. "The island was so wonderful. And everything will change when we get home."

"It doesn't have to."

"Correct me if I'm wrong, but the scenery will be awfully different." Her look was wry. "The lake is beautiful but it's not the ocean. And the pines are awfully pretty, especially against a clear blue sky. But they're not palms."

He knew when she said "different" she meant their relationship, and talking about the scenery was a way to avoid the subject. "We haven't discussed you and me."

"What?"

"Us. We haven't talked about what will happen with us when we get home. And I think it's time to do that."

"You do?"

"Way past time and completely my fault," he allowed.

"I wasn't sure there was an 'us.'" The hint of a sparkle was in her eyes.

"Well, there is." He took a sip of wine. "In case you couldn't tell, being with you was the best time of my life."

Her lips slowly curved up, the first genuine smile in almost twenty-four hours. "It was?"

"Without a doubt. And even though you're deserting me and Hart Energy, we will still see each other when we get back to real life."

"We will?" Suddenly she glowed with happiness.

"Yes."

Cal knew he couldn't *not* see her. He'd spent every day of the last four weeks with her. Every morning he saw her beautiful, serene smile and had breakfast with her. At night she curled up against him and he was filled with the passion of keeping her at his side, safe and happy. Somehow that kept him safe, too.

Tension seemed to flow out of her. "So do you want

to drink to cashing in on the bet with your brother? You did stay on the island for a month."

And she'd been with him during that time—first with work, then with her body. "That isn't my top priority."

"What is?" she asked, smiling.

He'd never brought up the future because he didn't know what to say. He hadn't thought about much of anything beyond wanting her with every fiber of his being. But now the future was staring him in the face and he wanted to do this right, be as honest as he could be. He had to put all his cards on the table.

"Justine—" Her name was a whisper on his lips and he leaned over to kiss her. Her mouth was warm and giving. "I care for you. A lot. And I want us to see each other when we get back to Blackwater Lake. But it's not fair to you not to be straight. I can't make any promises. What we have is fantastic. But I'm not very good at marriage."

"No one said anything about marriage." There was the barest flicker of change in her expression.

"I know. But it's important to be completely open about expectations and feelings."

She didn't make a sound. It was as if the light in her eyes dimmed. "Yes, it is. And I remember very clearly what you said about your feelings regarding marriage."

"Right." This was going better than he'd hoped. He was glad she understood. "I mean, who marries the woman who was in love with his brother, you know?"

"A competitive man," she said almost absently. "You want to come in first. It's what made you take the bet to spend a month on an island."

"Exactly."

"And I also remember you saying that you're not good at love. That you don't do anything that you're not good at."

"You have quite the memory." But Cal studied her closely after detecting something in her voice. "You say that as if it's a bad thing."

"That wasn't my intention. It's good to know one's strengths and weaknesses. Saves a lot of time and trouble. Good talk, Cal." She picked up her wine and took a sip, then stared out the window.

Somehow Cal felt as if he'd just made things worse and wasn't sure how. But clearly her sass had disappeared again. He'd fixed it once and could do it again. He would come up with something by the time they landed in Blackwater Lake.

Chapter Thirteen

The wheels of the plane touched down at Blackwater Lake Regional Airport. It was a smooth landing but Justine felt a jolt all the way to her heart. She'd wished the flight could go on forever. Just Cal and her cruising through the clouds.

That's what she'd been doing for the last couple of weeks, since the night she'd challenged him to take her to bed. Was it so awful to want sun, sand, seduction and sex to go on forever? There'd been no promises or declarations made, not until this plane had taken off and they started the trip home.

Cal had said he cared for her very much. It had been on the tip of her tongue to say that she was in love with him, so his statement made her feel...empty.

The Gulfstream taxied to the small terminal and stopped. Then the engines powered down.

"We're home." Cal smiled and released his seat belt.

"Yes." There was no point in disagreeing with the obvious.

But home? She hadn't lived there long enough to get all warm and fuzzy about it after being gone for a month. And then there was what happened with Cal. Not his fault, not anyone's fault that they were in different places. But she was going to quit her job and open her own business as soon as possible. She'd get it up and running, meet people and be happy in spite of him, damn it.

Tears filled her eyes and she didn't want Cal to see. That would be awkward. He would feel bad and she didn't want him to because she appreciated his honesty. Her life experience had made her who she was today and so did his. It was what it was.

So after freeing herself from the seat belt, she stood and turned away from him to look out the window. It was dark outside. Airport lights illuminated the immediate area where the plane was parked, and she could see into the terminal, which was all but deserted at this hour. There was a ghostlike air about the place, which felt appropriate, given her mood. The termination of hope wasn't a cheerful thing.

All she had to do now was keep it together for the next few minutes while collecting her luggage. Shanna had promised to pick her up. So a quick goodbye to Cal and she could be on her way to her apartment.

The flight attendant opened the rear door and chilly air swept into the cabin.

"It's cold out there," Cal said. "Welcome to Montana in November."

"Yeah." She looked down at her short-sleeved T-shirt and linen slacks. "A month ago the cold wasn't a priority and it never crossed my mind when we left the villa."

She'd been too preoccupied about where their relationship would go after returning to Blackwater Lake. He'd answered the question not long after the plane took off.

"The bags will be unloaded in a couple of minutes," he promised.

"Great." She smiled brightly and realized her jaw hurt.

That's what happened when you sat next to a man for hours and forced yourself to be cheerful when all you wanted was to curl into the fetal position.

"You stay here while I go check on things. Give me a couple of minutes."

"Okay."

When he headed for the open door, she texted Shanna that the plane landed. Her friend replied that she would be there ASAP. Then Justine gathered the personal items she'd kept with her and headed for the exit and climbed down the portable stairway that had been rolled into place. Cal was waiting for her at the bottom. He pulled a fleece-lined jacket around her. It was big and obviously his.

As if reluctant to break contact, he curled his hands into the material and held the coat around her. "You were awfully quiet on the flight. Are you okay?"

"Of course." The muscles in her jaw protested when she smiled.

"I'm not sure I believe you."

She was aware of his attention to detail, but had once again underestimated his powers of perception. "Oh?"

"I feel as if something I said is bothering you. Let me fix it."

She shook her head. It wasn't what he'd said that troubled her, because the truth was always preferable to being strung along. She blamed herself for disregarding the voice in her head that kept warning her not to cross the line from professional to personal with her boss. There were the obvious reasons, but he'd been open and upfront about his own past, the personal baggage he would always carry. She'd thought it was so sweet and sensitive when he'd held back his attraction for her sake. That was irresistible. And a mistake on her part not to resist.

"You didn't say anything wrong," she assured him.

There was enough light to see the questions in his eyes, but he nodded. "Okay, then."

"Good." This was the hard part. "I really enjoyed working with you."

"We do make a good team." His smile turned sexy. "And I'm not only talking about the work. We're very good together, Justine."

"It was a magical couple of weeks." The effort to keep her tone light and carefree took an enormous toll on her emotional reserves. "I'll never forget it."

"Me, either." He dropped his hands from the jacket and glanced over his shoulder. "I have a car waiting. I'll just tell the driver to load up our bags. Then we'll go to my condo and get settled."

Justine didn't know whether to kiss him or slug him. "Why would you assume that was okay with me?"

"You just said we're good together. We had a great time on the island and it doesn't have to end."

So sweet and yet so clueless. "You didn't ask, just assumed that I would be okay with this."

"I knew it." He frowned. "There is something wrong. Don't tell me you're fine when I know you're not."

"I think it would be best if we just—"

"Here's what I think." He took a breath and his lips moved as he silently counted to five. "Come to the condo with me. We'll sit in front of the fireplace and get warm. Have some wine. Hash things out."

There was a disaster scenario if she'd ever heard one. In a setting like he'd just described, their mouths would get busy, but not with talking. One kiss and she would be lost. Then all her clothes would come off, and for a while loving him would make her forget why getting in deeper would hurt so much more in the long run.

"I can't do that. I'm going to grab my bags and go. To my apartment."

"How are you getting home?" he asked, his tone rife with disapproval and irritation.

"Shanna is coming."

"The car is here. We'll drop you at your place. Tomorrow night we'll have dinner together and—"

"No."

He stared at her, apparently shocked into speechlessness at her negative reply. Finally he said, "That's it? No explanation?"

"How about this?" She thought for a moment, trying to figure out how to say this without crying. "The island was fantasy. It's over. Parting ways makes the break quick and clean."

He frowned and his mouth pulled tight. "What if I don't want a break?"

"I think you do," she said.

"And why would you think that?"

Because you're competitive, she thought. He broke his leg and stayed on the island in spite of it because he was determined to always come in first. That would come between them eventually, just like it had with his first wife. Justine had once loved another man but it made her all the more certain about her feelings for Cal.

On the island he'd taught her that she was a woman who needed to give and receive love. She was afraid the love she gave him would never be enough because he would always feel as if he'd come in second place.

"Relationships shouldn't be a competition with preconceived ideas and regulations." She met his gaze. "I think even you would admit that I have the more compelling reason to shy away from anything permanent."

"And I get that, so—"

She held up her hand. She was so close to tears and couldn't last much longer. She needed to get this out while her composure would hold. "Let me finish. I'm not saying I ever want to fall in love and marry again, but I'm not about to shut down the possibility. You're laying down ground rules before the starting gun even goes off."

"I told you I want to see you." He was irritated and oblivious.

"And for someone else that might be enough." She studied him, memorizing every line in his face and the curve of his jaw. How she wanted to touch him, but that couldn't happen. "I know what it feels like when life pulls the rug out from under you. After losing my family all I could think about were the things I didn't do because of being tired, practical or selfish. I could have read to my daughter just a little longer when she was trying to delay going to sleep. I could have gone on that camping trip instead of arguing that it was less work to stay home."

"I'm not going to let you down," he said.

"I know you believe that, but it's not what I heard you say. I came alive again on the island and will be forever grateful to you for that. But you set limits, and I promised myself that I won't live my life with parameters."

"Justine, listen to me."

"No. I have to do what's best for me." She stood on tiptoe and pressed her mouth to his. The hardest thing she ever did was pull away from him. She slid his jacket from around her shoulders and handed it back to him. "Goodbye, Cal."

She took one last look at him, and when her vision began to blur with accumulated tears, she turned and walked away.

* * *

Cal had been back in Blackwater Lake for a week
when his brother Sam called and asked to meet at the
local pub, Bar None. He was on his way there now. Linc
was coming, too, and their cousin Logan Hunt had succumbed to Sam's arm-twisting to meet them. The Harts
were planning to kumbaya the guy, convince him that
they were family, not jerks like his father.

The problem was that Cal wasn't in a kumbaya kind of
mood. When Justine told him they were over before anything really got started, he didn't take her completely seriously. He figured she was tired from the long flight. Her
bad leg might have cramped up. His did. There could have
been any number of things bugging her, and he would
call to smooth over any rough edges of their parting at
the airport. So he tried to get in touch but had only been
able to leave messages, none of which she'd returned.

That in itself was a message. Over and out. He got it
loud and clear. Guys' night at Bar None worked for him
because it would involve a beer. Or ten.

He saw the familiar neon sign with crossed cocktail
glasses and turned left into the lot next to the rustic building. The parking area was only half-full. Monday was ladies' night and usually standing room only. But this was
Tuesday, and as far as he could tell there was nothing
promotional going on. Since they were trying to recon-
nect with Logan, quiet was probably better.

He parked the car and got out, then walked to the
heavy front door with a thick vertical handle. He let himself in and was swallowed up by the smell of peanuts,
burgers and beer. He spotted Linc and Sam at a bistro
table close to the bar. Apparently their cousin hadn't arrived yet.

The muscles in his injured leg were building up again

fast and his stride was strong, stable as he walked over. That was a relief because he didn't want any questions from them leading to things he didn't want to talk about. Plastering a wide smile on his face, he shook hands with his brothers who stood to greet him with bro hugs.

He and Sam were close in height. Linc was an inch or two shorter and his eyes were darker. In spite of the fact that he had a different father, they all shared the bond of growing up Hart. Now that he'd reconciled with his bride, Linc was the picture of a blissfully happy man.

"Hope you haven't been waiting long," Cal said.

"Just got here." Sam grinned. "The first round of drinks is on me. Because I'm the oldest brother."

Cal looked at Linc. "We should let him buy every round."

"Works for me," the other man said.

"Ah, sibling rivalry on display." Sam sighed. "Speaking of that, how was your vacation?"

"Great." Things didn't go sour until he got back to Blackwater Lake, so technically, that was the truth.

"You went to an island resort, right?" Linc studied him. "Is it just the light in here or do you not look very tan?"

"Now that you mention it…not very rested, either," Sam said. "And wasn't that the whole point of getting away? By the way, we'll settle up the bet at a to-be-determined time and place."

"Okay. And just so we're clear, I'm new at the whole vacation thing." Cal remembered Justine's approval that he had finally jumped into the spirit of it. The pain of simply thinking about her sliced through him and he vowed not to do that again. "No one warned me about having to work twice as hard to catch up on the work I didn't get to while I was gone."

That was mostly true. Work here at home had piled up. And now it was time to turn the conversation away from himself. He took one of the empty chairs, and the other two sat down again.

"You two look great." His brothers radiated calm and happiness, Cal noticed. He was pretty sure they wouldn't see that in him.

"Life is good," Linc said.

"How's Rose? Surely your wife has seen the error of her ways and wants that divorce, after all." Cal hoped his tone conveyed that he was joking. His downer mood made it hard to tell if he pulled it off.

"No." His brother didn't rise to the bait. "I would cut off my right arm to make her happy."

"Wow." Cal nodded and met his older brother's gaze. "And Faith? Is she regretting her decision to marry you yet?"

"Well, she leaves me notes all the time, on the little cards that go out with her flower arrangements. This morning I got one that said, 'Roses are red, violets are blue. Sugar is sweet and I can't wait for tonight.'"

"That doesn't rhyme," Cal pointed out.

His brother smiled, the look of a happy and satisfied man. "It doesn't have to. I got the message."

"We are lucky men," Linc said.

"Amen to that." Sam looked toward the bar and raised his hand. "There's Delanie. Let's get this reunion started."

The curvy, auburn-haired bar owner walked over to the table. "Be still my heart. I swear three such good-looking men make my knees go weak."

"Linc and I are already taken. Sorry, Delanie." Sam didn't look sorry at all. "But Cal isn't spoken for yet."

Cal knew Sam was kidding, but it didn't change the frustration and anger coursing through him. A rush of conflicting emotions made him want to pop his brother, but a move like that would generate a lot of questions that he didn't want to answer.

Cal smiled his most charming smile at the bar owner. "I am happily single and wear it with pride."

"Good for you. I expect to see you in here next Monday for ladies' night. My sister will be here."

"Didn't know you had one." Cal suddenly realized he didn't know much about her at all.

"I didn't know about her until a year ago. My dad had a secret." Her mouth pulled tight for a moment. "But I always wanted a sister and she has a little boy. Owen. I'm an aunt."

"Then we'll drink to that. Family," Sam said and looked around the table. "That's why we're all here."

Delanie followed his gaze and noticed the empty chair. "Are you expecting one more?"

"Our cousin, Logan Hunt."

She nodded and looked at Cal. "You'll have a bachelor buddy."

Thank God, he thought. All this marital bliss made him want to put his fist through the wall. The door opened just then and the man in question walked in and looked around.

"And here he is now." Cal waved his cousin over, not that he was anxious for backup or anything.

The man was in his thirties, tall, broad-shouldered and serious. He ran a successful cattle and horse ranch just outside the Blackwater Lake town limits. The only time Cal had seen him in anything other than cowboy boots, jeans, a snap-front shirt and a Stetson was at Linc's wedding, in a suit and tie.

There was wariness, not warmth, in his face as he walked over to them. The cowboy looked as if he'd found a knot in his favorite calf-roping lariat. But he'd shown up. That was something, right?

He stopped at the table and nodded at his cousins, then looked at the bar owner. "How are you, Delanie?"

"Good. Nice to see you, Logan. Your timing is perfect. Saved me a trip back over here to see what you're drinking. I'm taking orders now. What'll you all have?"

"Before you answer that," Cal said to the newcomer, "you should know that Sam is buying the first round."

Logan didn't crack a smile. "In that case, I'll have the lobster."

They all laughed and it broke the tension. Until then Cal had been aware only of his own black mood regarding the situation between him and Justine. Damn, there was that knot in his gut again, followed by a sharp pain in his chest.

"If you want lobster," Delanie said, "I recommend that fancy new restaurant up at Holden House. Here in my place I'm proud to say you'll get a really good burger, fries and beer."

"I'm in," Logan said.

The others agreed, and Delanie brought a pitcher and four chilled glasses before going to the kitchen to order up the food.

Sam poured, and when they all had a beer he held his up and said, "I'm glad you decided to join us, Logan."

The man touched glasses with them but didn't look too happy about it. "To be honest, I'm not sure why I did."

"Look," Sam said, "it's no secret in the family that our uncle, your father, is…"

"A womanizing, treacherous, deceitful jackass is the description you're looking for," Logan said.

"I wouldn't have put it quite that way," Sam said diplomatically.

"Doesn't matter how you say it. That's the truth." Logan looked at each of them, daring anyone to deny what he'd said. "He cheated on my mother and had children with more than one of his mistresses. When my mom had enough of it, she left, even though she had nowhere to go and no money of her own."

"I'm not sure if you're aware, but my father reached out to her. My folks wanted to help her any way they could—money, a place to stay. You're family." Sam's voice was steady but serious.

This was one time Cal was glad not to be the oldest. Glad to hang back and listen while Sam explained how their parents had reached out to the mother of four children, only to be turned down.

Logan nodded. "She was proud and humiliated by what he'd put her through. And frankly, she didn't want anything from Foster's family. She didn't trust anyone with the last name Hart."

"I get the feeling she's not the only one," Linc commented. "And before you get defensive, you should know that Hastings Hart isn't my biological father. He has many faults, but turning his back on family isn't one of them."

Their cousin looked surprised for a moment, then nodded. "We lived in the car for a while before Mom finally went to my grandfather here in Blackwater Lake for help. It's why we ended up here, and the old guy had warned her not to marry Foster Hart in the first place."

"Sounds rough," Cal said. Worse than rough.

There was a whole lot of agreement in Logan's hard expression. "It's why I legally changed my last name to my mother's maiden name. So I'm not particularly willing to claim his family."

"That's the whole point of us being here. To prove

we're not like your father," Cal said. He looked at his brothers, who all nodded their agreement.

"How many times have you heard the saying that the apple doesn't fall far from the tree?"

"And sometimes the tree has one bad one but the rest of the fruit is fine," Sam said. "No offense, but your father is just one bad apple. We want you and your brothers and sister to know that the rest of the family is here for you, man. It's time to get that chip off your shoulder. Give us a chance to screw up before you cut us out of your life."

Logan looked at each of them in turn, taking their measure. Apparently the no-holds-barred words got through to the stubborn man. He nodded and said, "It's something to think about."

Delanie returned with a tray full of food and set identical red plastic baskets containing burgers and fries in front of them. "Ketchup and mustard are on the table. I left onion on the side in case any of you have plans later—if you get my drift."

"Rose appreciates that very much," Linc said. "And we know for a fact that Faith has something in mind. She left Sam a note this morning."

"Okay." The bar owner grinned. "Then I'll just leave and let the four of you have this testosterone zone all to yourselves."

Defiantly, Cal put the onion on his burger with a flourish and took a big bite. *Take that, Justine Walker.* He was a free man and didn't have to think of anyone but himself. But then he felt the emptiness open wider inside him. Taking a deep breath, he counted, then forced thoughts of her out of his mind. As he chewed, he watched Delanie working the room to check on her customers, polishing glasses behind the scarred bar. He thought about her testosterone remark.

"Do you think she's a spy?" he asked, still watching the bar owner.

The other three men looked at him as if he'd sprouted wings and a beak. But it was Sam who asked, "Are we talking Chinese or North Korean?"

"I meant for the women of Blackwater Lake." Cal had thought it was obvious. "Does she eavesdrop on male conversations and pass the information on to the ladies?"

"Now that you mention it…" Logan's eyes narrowed as he looked at the bar owner.

"Whether or not she is passing off secret information," Linc said reasonably, "if you don't say anything you wouldn't want repeated, there's nothing to worry about."

Sam finished chewing a fry. "Exactly. Anyone who wants to can listen in while I talk about being the luckiest man in the world. There's only one woman in my life."

"What about Phoebe?" Logan said.

"Okay," Sam amended. "Two women in my life. And that little girl is something. I'm proud that she chooses to call me Dad."

"You should be." For the first time since walking in the door, Logan smiled. "Phoebe is a tough crowd."

"That's right. Faith told me she went out with you," Sam said.

"Yeah. Just a couple of times. We're just friends. There was never a chance of anything serious between us," their cousin said.

Having so recently been shut down for his aversion to marriage, Cal detected a certain tone in the other man's voice. "Why is that? How did you know for sure?"

"Because I proposed one time, to the mother of my daughter. She laughed in my face. The thing is, I didn't take offense. It was a relief and proof that it would have been a mistake. I don't ever plan to get married." He took a sip of his beer then smiled at their shocked expressions. "It's all good. She understood me and knew we were better off as friends. And now she's engaged to a great guy and I wish them all the happiness in the world."

Cal held up his half-empty beer glass. "I'll drink to that. A woman who understands."

"No female entanglement." Logan touched his glass to his cousin's.

Cal took a drink, sealing the male bonding vow to avoid messy man/woman situations even though he knew his reaction was for nothing but show.

Studying him, Sam had a skeptical expression on his face. "What did you do on vacation?"

"I was away from here." Cal wasn't sure whether or not his tone was defensive.

"Can't argue with that," Sam said. But he didn't look convinced that nothing had happened.

That's because something *had* happened. Cal had a sneaking suspicion that a month on the island had entangled him. He could drink beer, swear up and down that he was happy as a clam alone and put onion on his hamburger until hell wouldn't have it. But none of that changed anything.

When Linc and Sam left here tonight, there were women waiting at home for them. And Sam had something in writing to put a twinkle in his eyes. The truth was that when he and Logan got home they would be alone. It cut him deep and he realized how much he missed Justine.

Looking at his cousin was like looking in a mirror, and Cal didn't particularly like what he saw. A man who put restrictions on the future without giving the present a chance. Justine was right about Cal. He had a feeling he'd blown it with her big time and there was nothing he could do about it.

For a man who was into fixing things, that was a bitter pill to swallow.

Chapter Fourteen

After work, Justine bustled around her cute, cozy apartment, putting last-minute touches on dinner for her friend Shanna. The evening would be bittersweet—catching up and saying goodbye. She decided to think about the sad part later and focus on the excitement of a girls' night and not missing Cal so much it hurt. After being with him 24/7 for the last month, there was a big hole in her life. It had been two weeks since that night at Blackwater Lake Airport, and any day now this acute emptiness would go away. She was sure of it. He'd wondered once if her being so optimistic was draining, and right now she would give him a resounding *yes* to that question.

Just in the nick of time there was a knock on the door, saving her from a pity party. She had one every night, but company coming meant it would have to be postponed.

She opened the door and her friend was there, holding a bottle of red wine. "Hi, you. Come in."

Tall, brunette Shanna bent to give her a hug. "I'm going to miss our girls-only dinners."

Justine wagged her index finger, a warning gesture. "No goodbye-ing until absolutely necessary."

"There are rules now?"

"My bad." Justine figured she'd learned from Cal. He was the one who put up roadblocks before the marathon started. "It's just that I don't want to say goodbye at all and putting it off works for me."

Shanna made a sad face before handing over the wine so she could take off her coat and hang it on the freestanding rack beside the door. "It's not like I'm going to the moon. California isn't so far away. When you're sick of the snow here, hop on a plane. In a couple of hours you can be on the beach."

The word *beach* made Justine think of the villa, helping Cal to hop over to the lounge in the sand, walking hand in hand by the ocean, making love in the pool. As always, a beautiful memory of him was quickly followed by an ugly stab of pain. She forced herself to focus on Shanna. This night was about her.

She took the wine into the kitchen and set it on the granite counter top. There was an electric opener and she used it to get the cork out of the bottle. "How far will you be from the beach?"

"Sand and ocean are Mark's backyard. He showed me pictures. So did his family. They all live nearby, very close-knit."

"It sounds perfect." She put a lot of enthusiasm into her voice, and that wasn't easy when her own life was a train wreck.

"Not perfect," Shanna said. "But really good. I don't want to be one of *those* friends. Someone who makes it sound as if she has it all. I know nothing is perfect."

"Hey, this is me. I'm your friend." Justine took two stemless glasses from the cupboard and poured wine into each, then handed one over. "You're telling me about a very wonderful turn in your life and I'm glad for you."

"I know there will be bumps in the road. Life isn't idyllic all the time. Stuff happens." She tilted her head as a sympathetic expression slid into her brown eyes. "Look who I'm talking to. You know this better than anyone."

"I do." Justine nodded. "Which is why I have a unique perspective that gives a lot of weight to the unsolicited advice I'm about to give you."

"I'm listening." There was an eager, intense look on her friend's face.

"Don't apologize for being happy. Embrace the moment and revel in it. Maybe stuff will happen. Or maybe you've been sprinkled with fairy dust or sneezed on by a unicorn and your life will be magically free of problems."

Shanna made a mocking sound. "Yeah. Right."

"The point is, enjoy this wonderful time and share the details with me. I want to know *everything*."

"Like?"

"Start at the beginning. How did you and Mark meet?"

"At the muster drill, before the ship sailed." She sipped her wine. "All passengers have to attend a meeting about what to do if there's an emergency. Mark and I were seated together. And we got into trouble."

"At a drill to avoid trouble? Sounds like you," Justine teased.

"I know, right? This is going to sound really corny, but when I saw him it was like being struck by lightning. Later he told me he felt the same way. We started talking instantly and didn't notice the announcement coming over the public-address system. We kept chatting and passengers around us gave us the hate stare."

"No surprise. Life and death."

"Yeah. A crew member chewed us out and we had to stay after school for a private tutorial."

"Then what?"

"We got a drink and were inseparable the rest of the cruise."

Justine gave her a look. "And by that you mean…?"

"He was either in my cabin or I was in his suite." She giggled. "Mostly his because—hey—it was the best cabin on the ship."

Justine pictured a villa on the ocean and the luxury that had awed her. She'd be lying if she denied it was nice, but that's not what made her heart hurt. Waking up with Cal was perfect, and not doing that now showed her the difference. This was one of life's crappy times.

"And now that you're home?" she asked her friend. "How do you feel being away from him?"

"Like part of me is missing." In spite of the words, Shanna still glowed. "But he feels that way, too. Three days after the cruise ended, he flew into Blackwater Lake to see me. He said he missed me terribly and he has a private plane, so there was no point in being miserable."

"I see." But the truth was that two people didn't have to be separated by geography to be unhappy. She and Cal lived in the same town, worked in the same building. Apparently he was avoiding her as much as she was him because their paths hadn't crossed. There was no way to know how he felt, but she was in misery up to her neck.

"I know what you're thinking." Shanna caught her bottom lip between her teeth.

Justine sincerely doubted that, but asked anyway, "What would that be?"

"You're thinking that we hardly know each other. That quitting my job and moving to California is a big risk and there's no safety net. That he might talk a good game and break my heart after I've given up everything to be with him."

"Actually, I wasn't thinking any of that."

"No?"

"I don't have to because you already have. You made your decision and you're one of the smartest people I know. So I was thinking that you are courageous for going after what you want. That's to be admired."

"Thanks." Tears sparkled in her friend's eyes.

Justine rounded the bar separating the apartment's kitchen from the living room and hugged the other woman. "Be happy, my friend. No one deserves it more."

"Back at you." Shanna sniffled.

She wanted to add that Shanna would never be alone because Justine would be there for her no matter what. But that would imply doubt about the move she was making and it's not what she meant. Justine would be there in good times or bad. Friends supported each other that way.

The timer over the stove sounded. "Dinner's ready."

"Smells good." Shanna sniffed. "Garlic. Something Italian."

"Good nose. Lasagna."

"Yum. What can I do?"

"Toss the salad while I make the bread," Justine said.

"Aye, aye." She saluted, obviously still in a nautical frame of mind.

A few minutes later they sat across from each other at the small round table in the nook adjacent to the kitchen. Their plates were loaded with food and Justine had re-filled the wineglasses. She held hers up. "To a bright future."

Shanna tapped her glass and sipped, then picked up her fork and took a bite of salad. After chewing she said, "I've been going on about my news. Sorry."

"That's okay." Justine would rather hear about her friend's happiness than talk about her own pathetic personal life.

"Apparently I'm not the only one making a move." Shanna cut a bite of lasagna and her fork hovered over the plate. "I heard that you gave your notice, too."

"Yeah, I did." She'd turned it into Human Resources the day before. But it was her impression that they kept things like that confidential. "How did you know?"

"Cal mentioned it."

Justine wanted to fire questions at her friend. Like, how did he take it? Did he seem okay or was he ticked off? Was there anything bothering him? But she held back and simply said, "Oh?"

"Yeah. It seemed as if you two were working well together on the island and…" Shanna's eyes were full of questions.

Justine shrugged. "I always planned to leave and open up the yoga studio. You know that."

"But I didn't think it would be this soon," her friend said.

"The money he paid me to go to the island and be his assistant made it possible for me to speed up my timetable."

"Still, I didn't know you were going to do this quite so fast. I kind of thought you might be my replacement. Not just anyone can deal with Calhoun Hart."

Dealing with him had turned magical after she nearly got fired. He was funny and caring and observant. Being with him never felt like work.

"He just needs someone who will go toe-to-toe with him. Not be intimidated by his intelligence and being all about work."

Shanna picked at her salad, then put her fork down. "The thing is, he's different since he got back."

"Maybe it's you, looking at him through the prism of being deliriously happy," Justine suggested.

"No. It's like he's broken." She held up a hand. "I know about the leg and that it's healed. I'm talking about something that wouldn't show up on an X-ray. A spark has gone out. I don't know how to describe it, but he's changed."

"Because he's losing you."

"He's a big boy, a professional. He knows better than anyone that I can be easily replaced." Shanna met her gaze. "I see the same thing in you."

"Really?" This woman was far too perceptive. Justine was going to miss her terribly. And, bottom line, she didn't want to talk about something that couldn't be fixed. "I don't know what to tell you. Except that I'm very excited about opening the yoga studio. It's been a dream for a while now and finally coming true. A chance to help others. In fact, I have an appointment in a couple of days with a real estate agent to look at space in the retail center near the new hotel and condos at the base of the mountain. Life is really good. So I'm not exactly sure what you're seeing in me."

"I would believe that story if I didn't know you so well. There was just a little too much enthusiasm in your voice. I don't buy it. And I'm not gullible. What happened between you and Cal on that island?"

"It's a blessing and a curse that you know me so well." Justine sighed and put her fork down. "We had a thing—"

"What?"

"I meant to say 'fling.' We agreed that's all it was. He learned to relax and find balance between work and fun. I taught him a breathing technique. And he..."

"What?"

He showed her the part of her that could feel deeply for a man who hadn't died. "I got to experience luxury overload. So I have a pretty good idea how your life will be—private jets, chartered yachts off Greece, houses as big as a small country. It's going to be great."

Shanna stared at her for several moments, then seemed to make a decision. "When you're ready to talk about it, I'm ready to listen."

Justine didn't deny there was a lot on her mind. She appreciated that her friend understood and respected what she was keeping to herself. It's why they'd connected so strongly. Reaching over, she squeezed the other woman's hand. "I know. Thanks. And remember, this night is all about you and your future."

"It's just that I want everyone I care about to be happy, too."

"You're sweet. Which is why I love you. And I hope with all my heart that this move to California and being with Mark will bring you all the happiness you deserve."

For the rest of the evening Justine managed to say all the right things. She truly meant all the good wishes but couldn't help feeling envious because Shanna had her Mark. Cal didn't belong to Justine but she felt as if she'd lost everything. Again. She loved him. She'd been absolutely sure of that when they left the island. Then he was honest with her and it changed everything, convincing her they wouldn't work.

She'd thought when the plane landed and she'd refused his offer to go home with him that breaking things off would take care of everything. It hadn't. She missed him and that wasn't going away. He had changed her and the change hurt.

A few days after the attempted bonding with his cousin Logan at Bar None, Cal drove to his brother's house after work to settle up on the bet. He turned right into an impressive neighborhood of large, stately homes with great views of the lake and mountains. Real estate was all about location and this was probably the best in Blackwater Lake.

Sam had lived in his big, empty house all by himself until the wildfire last summer had forced some local residents to flee their homes. Faith was one of the evacuees and had temporarily moved in with him. They fell in love. Her eight-year-old daughter, Phoebe, approved of the match and, as the story went, had a hand in matchmaking and getting the two adults together. While Cal was on the island, Sam and Faith honeymooned, leaving Phoebe with their sister, Ellie, and her family.

He drove into the curved driveway and parked, then turned off the car's engine. Glancing at the gorgeous, etched glass front doors, he took a deep breath before exiting the SUV. It didn't escape his notice that counting his breaths had become a habit since his month with Justine. Now he had to face Sam and this was Cal's moment of truth.

After walking up a couple of steps, he lifted his hand to ring the bell, but the door opened before he could. His brother must have been watching. Who knew he was so anxious to hand over the keys to the classic car?

"Hi." Sam looked past him to where the SUV was parked. "I thought you were going to get a ride over so you could drive the Duchess home."

"About that…" Cal met his brother's gaze. "We need to talk."

"What is it about those four words?" Sam frowned as he closed the front door. "It occurs to me that I don't like hearing them from you any more than I do from my wife. What's wrong?"

"Nothing. You'll like this, I promise—"

Before he could explain, eight-year-old Phoebe came running into the entryway. "Uncle Cal!"

He got down to her level and grabbed her up when she threw herself into his arms. "Hello, kid."

"Hi." She wrapped her small arms around his neck and squeezed as hard as a little girl could.

It felt pretty good. "How are you?"

"I'm gonna be a Hart." The blond-haired, brown-eyed little cherub looked proud as could be. "Sam's gonna be my dad. For real."

Cal grinned at her. "That means I'll be your uncle for real, too."

"I know." She hugged him again. "I can't wait till Thanksgiving next week to say what I'm grateful for."

"Right." The coming holiday had slipped Cal's mind. His thoughts had been too full of missing Justine to think about much of anything else. And he didn't even want to contemplate how empty Christmas was going to feel. "Is someone hosting the whole family for Thanksgiving dinner?"

"The location keeps changing." Sam's expression hinted at a level of excitement rarely before seen. "Ellie is pregnant."

"I know."

"She's been feeling pretty tired and still has some morning sickness. So, Faith was going to cook, but since—"

"Mommy's going to have a baby," Phoebe blurted out.

Sam didn't seem the least bit upset that the little girl beat him to the announcement. "It's true."

"That's great news." He smiled at Phoebe, her arm trustingly resting on his shoulder. "That means you'll be a big sister. Are you ready?"

"Yes. I hope it's a girl."

"Something tells me you have no preference." Cal

looked at his brother, who nodded. Then he set the little girl on her feet. He straightened and shook the other man's hand. "Congratulations."

"Thanks. But the point is that now Faith is fighting morning sickness. So Ellie swears she can pull herself together and do the cooking. Mom and Dad are here and will help. That's the scoop at the moment. Are you going to be there?"

It was a valid question given his track record of missing family events. In the past if something work-related came up he'd chosen that over family, but not now. Not since Justine showed him what a balanced life should be. And yet he couldn't seem to find his balance without her.

"Phoebe Catherine—" Faith walked into the room looking a little pale, but still beautiful. It was obvious where her daughter got her good looks. "Oh, Cal, I didn't know you were here."

"It's not good when she uses both my names," the little girl informed him.

"I heard about the baby," he said and hugged Faith. "You look beautiful."

"Thank you, but do not tell me I'm glowing. That whole pregnancy glow thing is a myth. I look like something the cat yakked up." She did glow, though, when Sam put his arm protectively around her. "We're excited."

Cal got a double whammy of envy and pain as he looked at the happy family. It was everything he wanted and would never have.

Faith turned a stern look on her little girl. "It's bedtime and you know what that means."

"But you were in the bathroom throwing up."

"Thanks for sharing," Faith said wryly. "That's not humiliating at all. And it still doesn't change the fact that it's time for your bath."

"But Uncle Cal is here." She glanced up at him, a whole bunch of pleading in those big brown eyes.

Cal took her mom's measure and sighed. "I'd like to help you out, kid, but I'm pretty sure your mom could take me. You're on your own."

Sam smiled his approval. "Smart move."

Phoebe thrust out her bottom lip in a pout. "Don't think I'm going to forget this on Uncle Appreciation Day."

"Is there such a thing?" Cal asked, not the least bit bothered by the threat.

"It wouldn't surprise me." Faith shrugged. "There's Short People Appreciation Day on December twenty-first, the shortest day of the year. Grandparents Day—"

"And Grandma and Grandpa Hart will officially be mine when I'm adopted," Phoebe said happily.

"The folks are excited about it. Mom once told me she wants and is expecting all of us to do our part and produce offspring," Sam confided.

Cal figured eventually his mother would notice that he wasn't doing his fair share in the kid department, but that couldn't be helped. Without Justine… He refused to finish that thought.

"Grandma likes to play checkers," the little girl continued. "Maybe she wants to come over and see Uncle Cal and we—"

"Nice try, Phoebs." Sam's voice was firm. "But you've stalled long enough. Your mom said it's time for bed."

"Okay, Dad. 'Night, Uncle Cal." She waved, then headed upstairs.

Bewildered, Faith shook her head at Sam. "I don't know how you get her to cooperate, but keep up the good work."

"That's my plan." He tenderly touched her cheek. "You doing okay?"

"I'll live. Soda crackers and ginger ale are my friends."

She looked at Cal. "Good to see you. I'll be back down after I get her settled."

He nodded and watched her follow her daughter upstairs. Then he met his brother's gaze. "You're a lucky man."

"I know." Sam was grinning like a happy fool. "Want a beer?"

"Yes."

They headed for the big kitchen with its giant island and stainless steel appliances. Sam opened the refrigerator and pulled out two bottles.

He handed one over. "So, we need to talk. You were supposed to get a ride over here. How are you going to get the Duchess back to your place?"

"I'm not." Cal noted that his brother didn't look completely surprised. "I worked while I was on the island and that's a violation of the spirit of our agreement. I can't take the car."

"Well, you're honest. I actually knew all about it," Sam admitted.

"You did? How?"

"You're relatively new to Blackwater Lake so there's something you should know. It's growing, but still a small town. People talk. Your assistant said something to someone about you needing a substitute for her—"

"But she was on a cruise." Even as he said it, Cal remembered what Justine had said about Shanna not being completely out of touch.

"Even on a ship there's internet and there are ports of call. Communication never stops completely."

"My bad. I won't make that mistake again." The mistake he'd made with Justine was so much worse that his lie of omission was hardly a blip on the emotional radar. "But I didn't fulfill the terms of the bet."

"You stayed on the island for a month. You won."

Cal shook his head. "It doesn't feel that way."

"Because of Justine." Sam leaned back against the granite-topped island and met his gaze. "Don't look so surprised. I just told you how fast and efficient news is in this town."

"Still—"

"And you were acting weird at Bar None. Your heart just wasn't in it when you drank with Logan to a woman who understands and no female entanglements. I knew something was up."

"As you probably already know, Justine filled in as my assistant while at the resort."

"Seems like it turned out to be more than work." Sam set his beer on the granite and folded his arms over his chest. "I think you fell in love and somehow you were an ass. Now she won't have anything to do with you. Am I somewhere in the ballpark?"

"How did you know that?" When Cal wasn't feeling miserable and hopeless he was kind of impressed with his brother's intuition. "You went through it, too?"

"I know because Linc did the same thing when he married Rose, then left her. Fortunately, while getting a divorce, they managed to figure out they were in love." Sam looked smug. "I, on the other hand, knew what I wanted and went after it. Even though commitment made me sweat."

"It's not just that. I'm not very good at marriage."

"Baloney. If you find the right woman you don't have to be good at it. It's all about taking a leap of faith." He pointed at Cal. "And that's not a pun because of my wife's name. You're gun-shy because you made one bad choice. It's that damn competitive streak of yours."

Justine had told him almost the same thing, that he wanted to be first. "I'm working on that."

"In the long run it's not even faith as much as knowing in your gut that a certain woman is the only one you will ever love."

"I know what you mean."

"Then do something about it," Sam said.

"It's like you're reading my mind."

Chapter Fifteen

Justine normally enjoyed being with her work friends at Bar None, but not tonight. It was her last day at Hart Energy and she'd hoped to slip away quietly, but her co-workers were having none of that. Especially after losing Shanna the week before. They insisted on having a going-away party for her. Now the four of them were sitting around one of the bistro tables having wine, and the other three didn't notice she wasn't talking much.

At least she hadn't run into Cal on her last day. Since coming back to town she'd been avoiding him and figured he must be doing the same to her since their paths had never crossed after returning from the island. Part of her had hoped to accidentally run into him but that hadn't happened. So obviously coming home had put an end to the fling. If he wanted her, she wasn't that hard to find. The logical conclusion was that he didn't want her.

That thought pulled the knot of pain in her chest a little tighter.

"So, tell me about the yoga studio." Amy Karlik was a blue-eyed blonde who worked in Human Resources.

Justine suddenly realized the table had gone quiet and everyone was looking at her. "Hmm?"

"Your yoga studio?" Mary Davis, a brunette, was young, a local hire and not a transplanted Texan. "How long until you're open for business?"

"I finally found a location in the new retail center at the foot of Black Mountain. It's not far from the new hotel and condo development. I had thought it was out of my price range, but Carla, my real estate agent, did a little digging and found out it's in my budget."

"Cool."

"I want to tap into the tourist population as well as residents of Blackwater Lake. And it's strategically located—a reasonable distance from the heart of town and the resort. Prime location at an amazingly dirt-cheap price."

"Sounds perfect." Sherry Ferguson nodded her approval. "When do you think you'll be able to open?"

"I have to sign a lease first. The owner has been hard to get hold of, according to Carla."

"So you've never met with the person who owns the property?" Mary asked.

"No. Apparently he travels a lot and is difficult to pin down. There's been a lot of phone tag and faxing. But tomorrow I'm going to put my name on the bottom line."

"Let's drink to that." Amy held up her glass and the rest of them tapped theirs against it. "But without a regular paycheck, isn't it a little scary? You'll be on your own."

"No." Justine had been on her own for a while now. Then Cal had infiltrated her heart. Look how that turned out. Alone was better. She'd handled it once and could do it again. Now that she was out of his office there wouldn't be any danger of running into him unexpectedly. That thought should have been a relief, but it was just sad. Then it sank in that her friend had asked a business question, not a personal one. "I've got a financial plan carefully worked out by my accountant."

"That's so exciting," Mary said.

Funny, Justine had anticipated this moment being much more exhilarating than it was turning out to be. But now her life was defined by before the island and after. Since coming home, everything felt dull and drab. It didn't feel as if there was anything to look forward to. Not like at the villa when she couldn't wait to see Cal for coffee in the morning and the day was bright and shiny with promise. The prospect of a whole day with him for work and meals stretched in front of her.

She'd gone to the mat on not working overtime, but she would give almost anything to break that rule now and spend as much time with him as possible. Then she wouldn't have to put on a happy face because genuine joy would fill her and would show on the outside.

"You are excited, right?" Mary asked the question but all three were giving her funny looks.

She put her happy face firmly in place because anything else would require an explanation and she wasn't willing to talk about what was wrong. "This is a dream come true for me. Of course I'm excited."

"Okay. Good. It was hard to tell for a second there," Amy said.

"I just have a lot on my mind."

"Of course." Sherry nodded enthusiastically. "There must be a million things to do."

"Probably more like two million," Justine agreed. "And tomorrow is step one."

The other three fell into a conversation about the upside of having a friend in the fitness business, discounted rates on classes and nutrition counseling. Justine listened and interjected when appropriate. The women laughed when they were supposed to so she was pretty sure the right words came out of her mouth. But her thoughts kept wandering to Cal and his determination to avoid marriage. If only he had an open mind. Without that there was no point in investing time and energy.

Unexpectedly, tears stung her eyes. This was supposed to be a happy send-off for her, and letting her friends see that she wasn't in a celebratory mood couldn't happen.

She dipped her head and told them, "I'm going to the ladies' room."

"Should we order you another chardonnay?"

"That would be great."

She slid to the floor and walked past the long, scarred wooden bar where Delanie Carlson was polishing glasses. The place wasn't very busy.

Justine moved into the short hallway with two doors side by side. One said Gents and the other sign said Ladies. She walked through that one and went into a stall, then locked herself inside. Gathered tears trickled down her cheeks and she tried not to generate any more. Her eyes would get red and puffy; her nose would run. Not only was that an unflattering look, it would be impossible to hide.

"Darn it. Why you, Cal Hart?"

This just wouldn't do. Sooner or later she'd have to come out or her friends would notice.

"Pull it together, Justine." She took a deep breath, then unlocked the door and walked over to one of the four pedestal sinks with the old-fashioned white water handles marked Hot and Cold in solid black letters.

Looking at herself in the oval mirror she thought she'd nipped the meltdown just in time. She washed her hands and put a wet paper towel on her eyes, then checked her appearance one last time and took several cleansing, steadying breaths.

"Good to go," she said.

She walked the short hall and came out into the main

room. Delanie Carlson happened to be standing at that end of the bar. Justine smiled at the woman.

"Hi." The bar owner studied her, then frowned. "You okay?"

So much for being good to go. "Don't I look okay?"

"Honestly?" Delanie's auburn ponytail moved from side to side when she shook her head. "No. You've been crying."

"How did you know? Are you psychic?"

"Hardly." She laughed. "But people are my business. I serve drinks and food and make conversation. You don't work at this as long as I have and not develop an intuition. I've been watching you and I could tell something was off. Then you went to the ladies' room for a cry."

Justine glanced at the bistro table where her going-away party was going on without her. The three women were having a great time. "Do you think they noticed?"

"No."

"Good."

"So you don't want to talk to them," Delanie guessed. "But it won't be so easy to get rid of me because I know something's wrong. And you might feel better if you get it off your chest."

Justine doubted anything would make her feel better but figured she couldn't feel worse. "Okay."

The other woman waited several moments, then said, "Go ahead. I'm listening. Think of me like a lawyer. Anything you tell me is confidential."

She must have needed to talk about her feelings. Or maybe crying in the ladies' room had made her emotionally vulnerable, because it never occurred to her not to talk to this woman. There was no way to ease into this, so she plunged right in. "I spent a month on an island with Cal Hart."

"Oh?" There was surprise in the bar owner's voice.

"It was for work," Justine clarified firmly.

"Yeah, when someone talks tropical island the first thing I think of is work."

Okay, so more clarification was necessary. "He's a workaholic so his brother bet him that he couldn't take four weeks off and stay there. Cal had a schedule of aggressive physical activities planned to keep him busy and pass the time. But on the first day he broke his leg skydiving. He figured he might as well work, but needed an assistant to be effective."

"You?"

Justine nodded. "I was paid a lot. And that allowed me to put together the financing for my business faster than I'd expected."

"But?" Delanie put down the glass that she'd polished and slid her a wry look. "If there wasn't a *but* you wouldn't have been crying."

"Fair enough." Justine sighed. "We got close."

"You slept with him." It wasn't a question.

It was impossible to regret the pleasure-filled hours in his arms, but if she hadn't taken that step, her heart would probably be in better shape now. "Yes."

"Okay. Just wanted to confirm context. Continue."

"I hadn't thought it was possible for me to feel that way again." Justine explained about losing her husband and child and the long hospital stay followed by rehabilitation.

"That's awful. Really rough," Delanie said. Her eyes filled with sympathy.

"I can't even put into words how bad it was." She looked down at her clasped hands resting on the bar. "For a while I didn't want to live and felt guilty that I had. That feeling passed eventually, but I never expected or wanted to get close to a man again. Then I spent time with Cal and something shifted for me. I got what people meant about moving forward after tragedy and that finding personal happiness again wasn't a betrayal of the loved ones I lost."

"But?" Delanie gave her a *seriously?* look. "Again, I should remind you that I saw the crying."

"Yeah." She blew out a breath. "When we flew home, he told me he wanted to keep seeing me, but I should know he never wanted to get married again."

"And that was a deal-breaker for you." Again, it wasn't a question.

"Yes. I realized that it's important to me. It's who I am. And putting limitations on us was not something that worked for me. Doing that at the beginning doomed the relationship to fail."

"That's one way of looking at it."

"Is there another way?" The comment pulled Justine out of her pity party.

"Yes."

"Not for me." She shook her head. "I won't be putting myself out there again."

"The way I see it, that's a little like the pot calling the kettle black." Delanie met her gaze directly. "Now who's into limiting?"

"You think I'm wrong?" It was a little irritating to be judged. "I saw how suddenly life can be taken away. Wasting time doesn't work for me."

"It was only an observation and worth exactly what you paid for it." But Delanie hesitated a moment, then added, "I just wonder if you were looking for a reason not to take a chance on love again."

"I didn't have to look for a reason," she maintained, even as the words resonated.

"I'm just saying that you might be shutting the door on anything with Cal because you're afraid of being hurt again. And who could blame you?"

"Okay, then. And if he says up front he can't give me what I want—"

"Did it occur to you that he might just need time? A chance to wrap his head around what he feels before getting to a place where he wants what you want?"

Justine had every intention of pushing back about that, but there was a ring of truth in what the other woman said. Wow. She'd been so sure she had it all together and an open mind about going for it. She thought about Shanna, who was courageous enough to give up everything for a chance at love.

Justine wasn't even willing to invest a little time because she could be hurt and had shut Cal down flat. No wonder he hadn't bothered to track her down at Hart Energy. Now that she was out of there, no way would their paths cross. She'd preached not wasting time to the exclusion of a judicious investment of time. That philosophy was supposed to prevent heartache, but pain ripped through her. How ironic was that? Not taking a chance had resulted in a broken heart.

Justine drove into the Black Mountain Marketplace, which was directly across the street from Holden House, the new hotel. The recently opened retail center was already 95 percent occupied by high-end boutiques, a jewelry store, an organic food market and a juice bar. The business she wanted to open was the perfect complement to the stores already here.

Eventually she hoped to carry a line of fitness wear, but that was down the line. One step at a time. Hopefully she could come to an agreement with the property's owner on monthly rent and terms. She was getting a little frustrated on the length of time it was taking to finalize this deal.

Her Realtor was supposed to meet with the owner's representative but had gotten hung up, so Justine had wheedled the key from her. The woman was coming here as soon as she was available. Now that she thought about it, that was another perk of this small town. In Dallas no one would trust you with a key to anything unless they were there to supervise.

It would be good to go in alone and quietly study the space one last time, make sure this was what she wanted. More important, that it would work for her vision.

She parked in front of the Space Available sign in the front window, then exited her small, fuel-efficient hybrid sedan. Key in hand, she walked over and unlocked the door. Morning sun flooded the room, giving off a cheerful vibe in spite of the fact that it was empty.

There was wallboard up but no paint. It occurred to her that it was like a blank canvas on which to create her own vision. Now to come to terms with the owner on finishing it to her satisfaction. Apparently he had a contractor who would work with her in making the most flexible use of the area.

"Hello."

Justine whirled around and saw Cal standing in the doorway. "Dear God, you startled me."

"Sorry." He was wearing jeans, boots and a sheepskin jacket.

She'd only ever really seen him in shorts and cotton island shirts. But it was November and cold. The look was a good one, masculine and very Montana. Oh, please, who was she kidding? The man didn't have a bad look. Her pulse was pounding and skipping erratically. She was pretty sure she could concentrate on breathing and count her breaths, but the technique wouldn't calm her down or bring serenity. Not with Cal. She was so incredibly happy to see him.

"How are you?" she asked.

"Okay." He shrugged.

Was it wrong to be the tiniest bit happy that he was just okay? Not fabulous or fantastic, but only satisfactory? She wanted to think he missed her even a fraction of the way she'd missed him.

"How are you?" he asked.

"Okay."

"I guess yesterday was your last day at Hart Energy."

"It was."

His mouth pulled tight. "You won't be easy to replace."

Did he mean at the office or in his life? She'd given up the right to ask that question when she refused to give him time. She wouldn't blame him if he was the tiniest bit happy that she would never forgive herself for that. But if she knew anything about anything it was moving on.

"Leaving wasn't personal. I told you that," she said.

"You did." He looked around. "So this is where you decided to open your yoga studio."

Was that bitterness in his voice? She hoped not but felt compelled to make sure he understood. "It's better for the company to find personnel whose dedication matches your own."

"Funny thing about my dedication." He met her gaze. "Mine got a restructuring. A work/nonwork ratio reset. So when can I sign up for yoga classes?"

Her mouth curved upward, but she knew the smile was sad. "If you weren't ready for the change, you wouldn't have embraced it so enthusiastically."

"Maybe I had a good teacher." There was a breathtaking intensity in his eyes. "I'm sure you're going to be a very successful yoga instructor."

"I hope you're right."

"Of course I am. If you can make a convert out of me, you must be good."

She shook her head. "When you have visual aids like sea, sand and sky, it's easy to get the message across."

"I respectfully disagree." His gaze never left hers. It was as if he couldn't look at her hard enough. "You are the best visual aid."

This conversation was going in a direction that wasn't helpful for her peace of mind or serenity. She was here on business, and speaking of that…

"I have a question. Why are you here? How did you know I would be here?" She didn't know what to think, but one thing was for sure. "It can't be a coincidence that you showed up here at the same time I did to sign a lease on this property. What is going on, Cal?"

"That's three questions and a conclusion." He slid his hands into his coat pockets and moved closer, stopping just in front of her.

One baby step would put her body right up against his, and she wanted that so, so much. *Focus*, she ordered herself. "I'll give you another conclusion. This is very suspicious. And, of course, my real estate agent is conveniently not here. What are you up to?"

"Nothing nefarious, I promise." He sighed. "My brother, Lincoln, is in property development. He owns this retail center."

"Oh, I see. So you're here to break the news that it will be a cold day in hell before he would rent to me."

"Not even close." He smiled but it was tense. "I'm here to tell you that I rented this space from him and am prepared to sublet it to you at a lower cost."

It all became clear to her then. "So that's why the negotiations dragged on and the price went down to a number I would be crazy not to take."

"Yes."

"You would be subsidizing me." So much for everything being clear to her. "I don't understand. Why would you do that?"

"Don't go to the bad place, Justine." He put a hand on her arm as if he expected her to back away and run out of there. "First of all, your dream is a good one. Something to be encouraged."

And it would be realized. Her pride kicked in and her voice was defiant when she said, "I don't need any help, if that's what you're thinking. I can do this on my own."

"I agree. You're the strongest woman I know. And you'll do this with or without me. But you should know that if you decide it's without, I will still sign up for your classes."

"Why?" That was part suspicion talking and part hope, because the pleading look in his eyes was wearing down her pride, her defiance and her resistance.

"As it happens, the muscles in my bum leg aren't the only ones that need attention. Turns out the heart is also a muscle and needs regular exercise or it will waste away. It needs a good workout and you're the only one who can do that."

"I'm not sure I understand what you're saying." That wasn't quite true. She got it but was afraid to believe. "I could do with less muscle metaphors and more straight talk."

"You're right. My bad. So, here goes." He took several deep breaths. "When we got back to Blackwater Lake, my words were clumsy. In an attempt to be honest, I said it badly and should have just gone for the simple truth. I love you." He looked around the big, empty room. "This is your dream. But you're mine. I want to be part of yours in any way possible, but I'm really hoping you'll consider being a part of mine and marry me. If I had another chance, I wouldn't make a mess of it. I'm sorry."

"No, Cal. I am. It took missing you so much my heart hurt in places I never knew were there." She looked down, then back up and met his gaze. "I realized that I was too hasty and judgmental because I was looking for excuses to avoid getting involved. I was afraid of taking a risk and being hurt again."

"'Was'? Does that mean you're not afraid now?"

"I'm a woman who wants to love and be loved in return. You're my dream and I want one minute, hour, day or a hundred years with you. If you're sure—"

He touched a finger to her lips. "I've never been more sure of anything. I want to marry you, spend the rest of my life with you. Have children with you. We'll build our dreams together."

"That works for me. Where do I sign up?"

"Right here," he said, then kissed her for a very long time.

When they came up for air he looked into her eyes. "If it's all right with you, I'd like to marry you on Christmas Eve."

"Although that's very soon, it works for me. I've been

told that when you know you're in love, you just know. But I have to ask why?"

"Because the only present I want to unwrap on Christmas morning is my wife."

"That is so incredibly romantic." Her heart filled with love for this amazing man and there was only one right answer to his question. "Yes, I'll marry you on December 24."

She couldn't think of anything more wonderful than being his by Christmas.

* * * * *

Return to Blackwater Lake with
JUST WHAT THE COWBOY NEEDED
coming in January 2018 from
Harlequin Special Edition!

And don't miss out on previous books in
Teresa Southwick's
THE BACHELORS OF BLACKWATER LAKE
miniseries:

THE NEW GUY IN TOWN
JUST A LITTLE BIT MARRIED
A WORD WITH THE BACHELOR

Available now wherever Harlequin Special Edition
books and ebooks are sold!

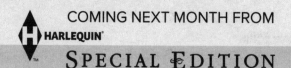

COMING NEXT MONTH FROM

HARLEQUIN

SPECIAL EDITION

Available November 21, 2017

#2587 MARRIED TILL CHRISTMAS
The Bravos of Justice Creek • by Christine Rimmer
Nell Bravo had her heart broken twice by Declan McGrath; she's not giving him another chance. But Declan has never forgotten her, and when they end up married in Vegas, he's determined to make it work. She'll give him until Christmas, but that's it. Will Declan be able to win her heart before December 26?

#2588 THE MAVERICK'S MIDNIGHT PROPOSAL
Montana Mavericks: The Great Family Roundup • by Brenda Harlen
Rancher Luke Stockton has been estranged from his family for a decade, and now that he's been welcomed home, local baker Eva Rose Armstrong warms his heart with her home-baked goods—but is he worthy of her love?

#2589 YULETIDE BABY BARGAIN
Return to the Double C • by Allison Leigh
When a two-month-old baby is left on Lincoln Swift's doorstep, the Wyoming oilman can think of only one thing to do—call old "friend" Maddie Templeton to come to the rescue. The next thing they know, they're caring for baby Layla and living together in Linc's home. But between the Christmas spirit and their strong attraction, this baby bargain might just result in love!

#2590 CHRISTMASTIME COURTSHIP
Matchmaking Mamas • by Marie Ferrarella
The Matchmaking Mamas are at it again, and this time they've arranged for Miranda Steele to get a speeding ticket from none other than Colin Kirby, a brooding motorcycle cop. He's determined to maintain his loner status, but can he resist Miranda's sunny charm and Christmas cheer?

#2591 A FORTUNES OF TEXAS CHRISTMAS
The Fortunes of Texas • by Helen Lacey
It's Christmas in Texas and another secret Fortune is coming home! Amersen Beaudin has left France to answer the summons of Kate Fortune, but when he meets lovely landscaper Robin Harbin, sparks fly. As Christmas approaches, can Amersen come to terms with his new family and own up to his love for Robin?

#2592 SLEIGH BELLS IN CRIMSON
Crimson, Colorado • by Michelle Major
Lucy is determined to get her life on track, and the town of Crimson, along with rough-around-the-edges rancher Caden Sharpe, soon become an important part of that. Her feisty spirit might be just what Caden needs to heal his emotional wounds. But when her past comes back to haunt them both, will their love be strong enough to weather the storm?

YOU CAN FIND MORE INFORMATION ON UPCOMING HARLEQUIN® TITLES,
FREE EXCERPTS AND MORE AT WWW.HARLEQUIN.COM.

*He may have broken her heart twice,
but Declan McGrath has never forgotten Nell Bravo,
and when they end up married in Vegas, he's determined
to make it work. She'll give him until Christmas, but
that's it. Will Declan be able to win her heart before
December 26?*

*Read on for a sneak preview of
MARRIED TILL CHRISTMAS,
the final book in* New York Times *bestselling author*
Christine Rimmer's *beloved miniseries*
THE BRAVOS OF JUSTICE CREEK.

"Why me—and why won't you take a hint that I'm just not interested?"

He stared into his single malt, neat, as if the answer to her question waited in the smoky amber depths. "I don't believe you're not interested. You just don't trust me."

"Duh." She poured on the sarcasm and made a big show of tapping a finger against her chin. "Let me think. I wonder why?"

"How many times do I need to say that I messed up? I messed up twice. I'm so damn sorry and I need you to forgive me. You're the best thing that ever happened to me. And…" He shook his head. "Fine. I get it. I smashed your heart to tiny, bloody bits. How many ways can I say I was wrong?"

Okay. He was kind of getting to her. For a second there, she'd almost reached across the table and touched his clenched fist. She so had to watch herself. Gently she suggested, "How about this? I accept your apology. It was years ago and we need to move on."

He slanted her a sideways look, dark brows showing

glints of auburn in the light from above. "Yeah?"

"Yeah."

"So then we can try again?"

Should she have known that would be his next question? Yeah, probably. "I didn't say that."

"I want another chance."

"Well, that's not happening."

"Yes, it is. And when it does, I'm not letting you go. This time it's going to be forever."

She almost grinned. Because that was another thing about Deck. Not only did he have big arms, broad shoulders and a giant brain.

He was cocky. Very, very cocky.

And she was enjoying herself far too much. It really was a whole lot of fun to argue with him. It always had been. And the most fun of all was finally being the one in the position of power.

Back when they'd been together, he was the poor kid and she was a Bravo—one of the Bastard Bravos, as everybody had called her mother's children behind their backs. But a Bravo, nonetheless. Nell always had the right clothes and a certain bold confidence that made her popular. She hadn't been happy at home by any stretch, but guys had wanted to go out with her and girls had kind of envied her.

And all she'd ever wanted was Deck. So, really, he'd had all the power then.

Now, for some reason she didn't really understand, he'd decided he just had to get another chance with her. Now she was the one saying no. Payback was a bitch, all right. Not to mention downright delicious.